Keeping the
Promises

Keeping the Promises

Dhruv Gajjar

Srishti
PUBLISHERS & DISTRIBUTORS

SRISHTI PUBLISHERS & DISTRIBUTORS
Registered Office: N-16, C.R. Park
New Delhi – 110 019
Corporate Office: 212A, Peacock Lane
Shahpur Jat, New Delhi – 110 049
editorial@srishtipublishers.com

First published by
Srishti Publishers & Distributors in 2015

Prologue

What comes to your mind first and foremost when you think of the greatest thing you've done for someone you love? There are so many books written on love, numerous romantic movies made on it. But can love stories ever be squishy and tragic at the same time? Well, yes. At least for us it was. Dhruv – once a naive schoolboy, who grew up with me – has lived every shade of love, pain, sorrow and everything in between at the age when boys almost puke at the idea of committing to someone for the rest of their lives. I wasn't around when he was fighting his life's worst phase, but I'm happy to be around now, helping him get at his best again.

When he met me for the first time after years, he was not merely a boy who was my best friend or someone whom I could call my first love. He was a man who had lost his meaning and reason to live. He was not a person who'd spend hours in the gym pumping his muscles – though back in our school, he was impeccably handsome... having the physique of an athlete, with facial curves capable of charming and intimidating anyone of the opposite sex. I have no hesitation in admitting that I was one of them. I loved him then as much as I do now. Few – let's say thirty odd extra pounds of his weight can't alter my feelings for him. He still beguiles me the way he used to back then. He hasn't changed from his heart and for that I will always be grateful to him. When I first met him after all these years, his mind was empty – without any motivation, hope or goal. To sum it all, he was messed up. There was nothing in this world capable of keeping his interest, except a task – a task of writing and publishing his book. I wouldn't be wrong if I'd say it was the only thing that was keeping him alive. It wasn't easy for him to write about the person he loved, and will love for the rest of his life, whose name he could not mention. Writing about her meant envisaging the entire screenplay, to relive the moments which were blissful and afflictive at the same time. But he had me beside him – holding his hand whenever needed, wiping his tears whenever required, and living the moments with him while hearing his narration.

This is the story of Dhruv and M. This is the story of Ansh and Angie, and at the same time, this is my story as well.

Ahmedabad

I am sitting at the Cafe Piano, TGB, the same restaurant where they used to meet. His MacBook pro and diary are placed on the table. We are not dating, not yet. I don't think we can head towards a relationship just like that and pretend that nothing happened – especially after all that he went through. We can sense the growing affection towards each other, but we can't go further with that, at least not now – not until he comes out of his despondent state of mind.

"So, finally you are starting it!" I say with a gentle smile in order to boost his confidence.

"Yes, but I don't know where I should start from," he answers, glancing at me with his confused, distressed face, whereas I'm sitting firm, smiling at him, and trying my best to help him fulfil his yearnings.

"Start it from the day you got to know about it Dhruv!" I suggest.

"Okay, let's start," he says and open his Mac; tears start rolling down from his eyes the moment he envisages the scene.

1 February

I crumbled on the floor as I saw her, an instant fling with the floor apparently pained me, but it was nothing compared to the pain looking at her caused inside. This was even worse than I imagined. She was lying on her bed, her body except her face was covered inside the white blanket. Her face was almost dry and pale, her glowing and well-nourished cheeks had wrinkled and dried too. Chemo sessions, that must be chemo sessions that had taken away most of her silky brown hair. She was still asleep.

So that's what she was hiding from the past seven months.

That's why she had asked for a break-up. She did not cheat on me. She was ill, and she didn't want me to know. But why? Was I not worthy enough to know about it? Why did she keep it away from me? I could've helped her. We could have given her the best treatment in the world. After all, I belong to a family of doctors. I heard the sound of someone opening the door; glancing up, I saw her father standing. He gave his hand to me because I needed some support to stand up.

"What is it, sir?" I asked with teary eyes.

"Neurofibrosarcoma."

"What? But she is too young for that! No one gets it at the age of twenty!" I was digging my brain to pull out the little information I had about the disease.

"That's where she was mistaken – by herself and by the local physicians," said Ansh who came from behind along with M's mother.

"You knew about this?" I snapped at him, with anger, of course.

"From the very beginning... In fact, everyone knew about it except you. Sorry bro, but I gave her my word like everyone else," he said and hugged me.

"Tell me that she is going to be fine, Ansh!" I didn't want his consolations; I wanted some answers, some assurance.

"I wish I could Gajju, but the fact is that she doesn't have much time left. She reached the final stage four months ago," he said, staring at his toes.

"What? That's impossible! No one can die in just seven months in any cancer! I'm calling my brother. We'll give her the best treatment in this world. She cannot die. She is going to live, she will have to!" I squeaked in pain. No one reacted; my outrage was righteous and expected.

"Not just seven months Gajju! She had it for one year before she was diagnosed. Besides, she has given up. She could have undergone surgical treatment or the radiation therapy, but refused to every alternative," he said with teary eyes.

"What? But why?" Tears had no destination and kept falling down, from not just mine but everyone's eyes…aimlessly, like a monsoon shower or dew drops of a frosty December morning.

"Neurofibrosarcoma has been a curse to our family. My father died with the same disease, even after having two limb surgeries. Before him, his two brothers and my grandfather too faced the same fate. At that time, we didn't even know that it was something called neurofibrosarcoma. And they died in their fifties. I thought that the affliction of the disease was over when I didn't have it, but…" M's father choked with his words. Though I knew little about Neurofibrosarcoma, I knew it could either be due to an unidentified cause or genetic. He took a gulp before finding his voice back. "She said she wanted to end the death streak here. We tried to force her a lot, but she was firm in her decision. She did not want to take this disease further. She is the youngest victim of this disease in our family. She saw it as an opportunity to end that torment here. She believes that she has sacrificed her life in this, but has saved many." I looked at Ansh with an overwhelming realm of pain in my eyes.

"Why Ansh? For god's sake, why M?" He embraced me as he heard this.

"I wish I had an answer to this, my friend."

There was a dark silence. I did not have anything more to question, they did not have anything to answer. Just then, she moved her head a little. Everyone else, knowing that it was my time to be with her, left the room. I quietly sat beside her, ran my hand on her almost bare forehead. She was true to her words about recognizing my touch even in her deepest sleep. She did, slowly. When she opened her eyes, I saw that the twinkles were still there; nothing, no cancer or chemo sessions could take that away.

"Hey beautiful!" I smiled with wet eyes. She broke into tears as she saw me. Maybe she'd noticed that her handsome hunk had turned into a fat pig.

"What have I made you, Mithu!" Hearing that word always made me smile and that day was no exception.

"Nothing baby, just gained some weight. As you lost some hair," I said and caressed her greyish hair.

"I was wrong. I thought you would move on. Dad told me I was wrong…I should've listened."

"Hey M, shhh!" I put my right index finger on her still pink panoptic lips. "Let's not talk about that! See, I'm with you now. That's the only thing which matters," I rubbed my hands on her forehead, wiped her tears which were back in no time. I wiped them again and they came back, again. Finally, I was the one to give up the effort and lost the battle with her tears.

"M? Is there any hope where we can start your therapy again and try to save you?" Her face frowned as she heard my words; she took a deep audible gasp and I felt every bit of her inhalation and exhalation.

"I've my reasons for doing this, Mithu! Maybe someday you'll understand, maybe not, but from here, it's irrevocable. I'm dying and no one can change it."

"I can! We can start your therapies again, and from now, I'll be here with you all the time, and I'll not let you die, understand?" I groaned, while she kept weeping.

"Understand, my love?" I raised my voice, as if I was challenging her death, which was nearby and could be arriving anytime soon. I realized I had been a little loud. Even her father had heard it, and swung the door open to come inside. I stood up.

"Sir, I would like to seek your permission," I softly demanded. Before I could even explain what it was, he answered me, as if he knew it was coming.

"You can stay here as long as you want son. You deserve the remaining time that is left with her and I would do every possible thing I can to help you in that."

I was dumbfounded by his guess. After gathering the courage to speak something, I uttered, "Thank you, sir. M, I'm going to bring my clothes and some other stuff. Wait for me, okay?" She nodded and I left the room.

Back in my house, I was packing my clothes and other necessary stuff when my father and brother came into my room.

"Where do you think you're going?" Dad scoffed.

I rushed towards them and hugged them both.

"Dad, Bhai! I know I've always been a troubled child for you two. I screwed up my life, jeopardized my career, but believe me, I need to go now. I can't tell you where I'm going, but I need you two to trust me on this. I know you have so many reasons not to trust me, but still, if you ever thought that I was good, please let me go. I promise I'll come back being better and stronger than ever," I said. I wasn't usually a crybaby. They had hardly seen me crying after puberty. They didn't say anything, nor did they oppose. I considered it an affirmation and took my bag and started to walk.

"Dhruv!" I heard my brother's voice from behind.

"Yes, Bhai?"

"Remember, if you need anything, and I mean anything, we are just one call away and I dare you to come back with my brother who used to be a better person." I nodded, smiled and walked out.

I reached her apartment. Her father was waiting for me – to lead me to his parking lot where I could park my car. I followed as he said and parked the car, took my bag from the side-seat and stepped out.

"Thank you, sir. I really appreciate what you are doing. I know allowing her daughter's boyfriend…"

I was still speaking when he interrupted me, "Son, she is my only daughter. Right now, we cannot afford the luxury of those negative thoughts; we all have limited time with her, so together, let's try to make it cheerful," he said and put his hand on my shoulder.

"We will, sir!" I firmly said.

"And I have a request! Call me dad from now on if you don't mind. We do not have the time to get you married with her but at least we can enjoy a father-son equation till you are here." He said with a smirk. I realized we shared the same pain, the same unbearable grief, the same heart-wrenching anguish. She didn't choose death over me; she chose death over us.

"We will dad!" I gently said and we both went inside.

As soon as I reached her room, I placed my stuff in her wardrobe, which her mom cleaned and emptied for me. I took out some orchids – her favourite flower – which I had bought specially for her.

"You are not moving in here permanently, are you?" She chuckled as she watched me from her bed.

"May be, who knows?" I replied with a wink.

"But what would I get in return to let you stay here?" She moved her eyes, as provocatively as she used to while teasing me.

"I can be your full time caretaker ma'am!" I meekly answered.

"Good! But, not enough! I want you to wake me up with these flowers."

"Checked!"

"Every morning, I need these orchids. Don't you dare wake me if you do not have them."

"As you wish, my blue eyed girl!"

"After that, your special omelettes! You'll be badly punished if I don't find it tasty, even once."

"Checked!"

"You will have to write a story for me, every afternoon when I go to sleep; do not waste your time by just looking at me. Make the best use of yourself, write a story for me and wait till we finish our dinner, which obviously will be cooked by you and only after that, you are allowed to narrate your story to me. If I find it boring, you shall be punished."

"That was unpredictable, but checked!"

"I'll take a promise from you, every night before we go to sleep, and you will keep it till your last breath, clear?"

"As crystal ma'am, checked!" I bowed on my knees.

"It's almost afternoon now, I'm going to sleep. There is a diary inside and an ink pen. You'll be pleasured to write with it. Now come here and do something useful."

She fell asleep. I didn't realize how the afternoon turned itself into an evening. I kept writing, not just any other story, but the story of our life. Words kept coming till I was sure that I had enough for the day. By the time it was already five, and she was still sleeping – quietly, in the world of her dreams. I put down the diary and held her hand. A girl, who meant my life, was on the verge of dying. She could have stayed, at least for a few more years, if she had her therapies or a surgical amputation of the infected limb, which I was yet to see. I was just observing her face, her only visible part. I was lost in her memories when her mom came inside.

"What will you have for dinner, son?"

"Auntie, you're going to make it now? Wait, I have been ordered to help you."

"It's fine son! Just tell me, what will you."

"You are not getting my point auntie. Your daughter will not see my face until I cook for her." I chortled; she guffawed, as she understood whose order I was obeying.

"As you wish son, let's go."

And I followed her to the kitchen. Dad was already waiting for us there.

"Three cooks for one person? My princess is apparently having a royal treatment," Dad chuckled.

"Yes, Dad! But let me take the charge now, what does she eat for dinner?" Seeing me call him dad dumbfounded her mother, but in a minute, she was delighted.

"Okay then, I'm sitting outside as it's the news time." He said and walked out. I asked her mother what usually she had for her dinner. She said that usually at nights, doctors had suggested only soup for her. They said it mattered a little now, but light food like soup could prevent her chocking due to foreign bodies. Her mother broke into tears. I found that not only dad and I, M had chosen death over her mother too.

I decided to make roasted garlic and tomato soup. As I always had a soft corner for cooking, it was going to be an honour as well as pleasure to cook for my girl. We checked the ingredients – tomatoes, garlic, onion which had to be chopped, bay leaf, salt, basil leaves, fresh thyme, tomato puree, crushed black peppercorns, white bread slices and basil oil. Everything was set. I then cut the tomatoes into big pieces while her mother chopped the onions in the chopper, then I cut a thin slice from the bottom of the garlic bulb, and placed it in a bowl to roast it in an oven until it turned brown.

"It smells good, now what?" Her mother asked as she pulled out the bowl.

"We need to heat two spoons of olive oil auntie!" I softly answered.

"Dhruv, it's quite unfair that you call my husband dad and me auntie?" She quipped with a smile. I realized we all had turned into eccedentesiasts – people who hide their pain behind their smiles.

"We need to heat olive oil, Mom!" I grinned, and she responded with a smile too. I thanked my God for blessing me with new parents.

She then heated the two-teaspoon olive oil in a non-stick pan. After it was heated enough, I added chopped onion, tomatoes and bay leaf in it. Then I sprinkled salt in it and mixed it until the mixture was ready for some garlic cloves in it. Then I added thyme and one cup of water to cook. It was now the time to add tomato puree and mix it, but not before adding basil leaves and crushed peppercorns in it. It was now tomato's turn to become soft and it took around ten minutes of covered cooking to do it. I then gently removed the strain and reserved the stock, not before removing the thyme and the garlic cloves from the solids. I let it cool and then ground it to a puree with a little water. I also added the bread pieces and ground once more. I poured the strained stock and the puree into the pan and brought it to a boil but not before adjusting salt, and the soup was ready. I poured it into a soup bowl and made it ready to be served.

I went out, and saw dad watching TV. When he saw me coming, he sensed that the soup was ready, and it was now the time to wake our princess.

"You will need this wheelchair," he said pointing his finger to the wheelchair on the side corner. The wheelchair was black; it had adjustable footrests, removable handrails, reclining backrests and head support. I placed my hand on the push handle and led it to her room.

She was still sleeping. I placed my hand on her forehead to wake her up. And she gently – just like a sunrise – opened her eyes.

"Wake up, my love!" She smiled as she heard me. I then uncovered her blanket to see it for the first time – I shuddered at what I saw. I knew it was there…had seen many cases in the ward, but seeing someone beloved like that was always unendurable. Her white salient legs had turned completely black, tumour cells had eaten all her muscles of lower-limb, like her calf, once well-toned by gastrocnemius and soleus were almost gone on her right leg . The swelling on her left thigh that had doubled its weight, comprised nothing but pus inside. Her tumour cells were on their way to the spinal cord where the metastasis would soon eat her bones, then her lungs and sooner or later, she would die choking. A doctor in me said it all, but the lover in me instantaneously refused and kicked his butt. Her transparent white gown was covering her abdomen and pelvis, which was yet untouched by the tumour cells.

"How's it?" She moved my attention with a smirk.

"Gorgeous, no one can clinch away your beauty, you know that," I winked.

"In our two years of relationship, you haven't praised me even half of what you are doing since morning," she kept her teasing going.

"I never knew you needed it," I retorted.

"You smart ass Mithu!"

"You sexy ass M!" And I bumped my head with hers.

"Now lift me up and make good use of your muscles," she demanded.

"They are gone M!"

"Ah, they will be back, don't tell me you can't lift me without them."

"I can try."

And I lifted her in my arms. It wasn't as hard as I thought. I still had something left in me. Marijuana and alcohol hadn't consumed all of me. I gently put her down on the wheelchair and slowly drove her to the dining room where mom had already placed the soup on the burnished table. Dad started rubbing his palms in childlike exuberance as he saw us coming. I took my chair and even though she could move her hands, she asked me to feed her. I picked up the glass spoon, filled it from the bowl and slowly fed her.

"It's delicious," she said with her miraculously twinkling blue eyes. I kept feeding her and myself until she finished the last sip. I then washed my hands and cleaned her face with a napkin. Mom and dad went inside to change her bedsheet. As she was in her final stage of dependency, she couldn't move her extremities. Dad instructed me that it was my job now to place her bedpan, to change her clothes and to wipe her back. After a brief talk, she told me to take her inside as she desperately wanted to hear my narration. I made a strong grip on push holder and took her to her room. As we reached, she raised her arms, wanting me to lift her. I gently lifted her from the wheelchair, placed her on the bed, adjusted her backrest and covered her infected legs with a blanket.

"What is it about?" she asked.

"About us!" I answered with a smile, stood up, took my diary, sat beside her and started reading.

Once upon a time, there were two best friends, Dhruv Gajjar and Anshul Bhatt. Anshul Bhatt belonged to a middle class family, had every quality of fitting in an ideal son's shoes. On the other hand, Dhruv Gajjar – called Gajju by his friends – was a highly irresponsible gym freak, who had no goals in his life other than to keep pumping his muscles. After coming out from admission counselling, Ansh should have been delighted for making his way into MBBS at SBKS medical college, Vadodara but he was rather sad for Gajju, since he hadn't gotten admission anywhere. On the first day, Ansh, along with his parents, entered inside Sumandip campus. There was a board signalling for the way to the parking lot. As they proceeded, they saw a long queue of cars heading towards the front parking lot. Audi, BMW, Mercedes, Porsche symbols were radiating with the morning light. Ansh wondered if they were the only ones with a Maruti 800. But in the parking lot they saw a few more cars like Zen, Santro, Maruti 800, Maruti-Suzuki Esteem and so on. He assured himself that he wasn't the only one to have secured admission on merit basis.

They parked the car and stepped out. They were informed to go to the hostel first and it was a long walk from the front parking lot.

"Dad, Mom! The hostel is about a kilometre's walk from here. It's okay if you don't want to come. I will get the luggage by myself," Ansh said. His parents had diabetes and he didn't want to trouble them with the long unnecessary walk.

"It's okay Ansh! We are still in our forties, not sixties," His dad quipped and they started walking. Outside the parking lot on the right hand side, there was a temple. Ansh's mom folded her hands to take god's blessings. His mom was totally into those religious things; there were innumerable 'vrats' and 'poojas' she held for Ansh to make it through and now, when he did – she was thanking god for accepting her prayers. After passing through the temple, they saw a few doctors waiting for an ambulance outside the hospital door, wearing white lab coats, hanging stethoscopes around their necks. Ansh felt enchanted knowing that someday, he will be doing that noble job of treating patients as well. Ambulances were coming and going in the frequency of every two minutes and guards at the gate had a well-separated special path for them. The hospital was big – surrounded by trees and plants to maintain the oxygen level. Then they passed through the medical college. The entrance was crowded by parents and their children; parents who were instructing their children and children who merely listening to them. On the backside, they saw the canteens and messes; smell of various eatables irritably lingered in the air, only then Ansh realised there was one thing he was going to miss the most – the food cooked by his mother. He then gazed at the buildings of the girls' hostels. They were more like three-star hotels in India. He could see the curtains on windows, exhausters of split air conditioners, clean and shining floor and pleasant surrounding. All this was exceeding Ansh's expectations that he was going to live in a likewise place, but when he saw the buildings of the boys' hostel, all his expectations dropped in a swish. They were no better than warehouses, with broken windows and faded coloured walls.

"Girls' hostels are better Ansh!" Ansh's mom said.

"It's okay mom! They always get the advantage," he gagged.

As Ansh was taking charge of everything, he asked his parents to wait outside the warden's office and went in.

"Hello sir! We are here for..." Before he could finish his sentence, he cut him off,

"I know, for room possession. Sorry son, but you'll have to wait for a while. Room allotments will take place in the evening," he politely answered.

"But sir, my parents are with me and I have bulky luggage."

"Don't worry about that. Let me talk to your parents," he said, settled his spectacles and stood up.

"Why the hell did I not send my parents first?" Ansh thought.

The warden walked out from his office and Ansh followed him. He shook hands with his father, "Sir, we are yet to get the full list of merit students and students from management quota. So, your son will be allotted a room in the evening. Keep his luggage inside the store room. You'll get a badge from a guard outside. Stick this badge with your luggage, write his full name and admission number on it." They followed everything he instructed and finished those formalities.

Then Ansh turned to his parents, "Dad-mom, you two should leave now. It will take two-and-a-half hours to get back to Ahmedabad and I want you to reach before afternoon! It will get hotter then and would trouble you to drive a non-AC car. I'm going to college now." Ansh said, keeping his ideal son image alive.

"Don't worry about us, son! We will be fine." Ansh's father said with a gentle smile and turned to his mom, "Let's go then!" Ansh's mom nodded. But since being a mother, she had to cry, she did. Only after calming her and seeing them off, Ansh went to college.

After having a completely absorbing first day at college, Ansh went to the hostel. He went to the storeroom first to get his luggage, but it wasn't there. The guard said that his room partner had already taken the possession of it, which made Ansh agitated. Fumed, Ansh rushed to his room and all his anger was gone in a swish when he met his room partner there.

"Gajju? What the fuck is this?" Ansh asked in astonishment.

"Ah, I just couldn't miss this million dollar expression of yours! That's why I kept it from you. Dad took my admission in NRI quota. Now get ready for a six-year long honeymoon baby!" Dhruv simpered.

"With pleasure, you Asshole!" Ansh retorted. They were extremely delighted with the way things were going. On the same night, they ascertained three new friends – Shilpan, Aakash and Harsh who were lodged in the same lobby and belonged to the same city, Ahmedabad.

"That's it?" She asked as I finished.

"Yes, for one day, it's adequate," I answered and reached her hands under the blanket.

"Since when are you and Ansh best friends?"

"Since the day we marked our footsteps in school."

"Hmm. Okay."

I gently rubbed her hands and took her in my arms.

"Now it's promise time Mithu!" she murmured.

"Your wish is my command ma'am!" I bowed my head a little.

"Promise me! You'll write a book on it and publish it."

"What? Baby, writing for you is a different thing and writing a book is entirely different. They are great with words and I neither have the writing skills nor the command over language or a good vocabulary to stand a chance," I said trying to be as truthful as I could.

"Don't grow sceptical on yourself, Mithu! I know things about you, which even you are completely oblivious of. Besides, our love story has to be conveyed and that would be your best dedication to me after my death." She squeezed my palm to provide the faith I needed at the first place.

"Okay, I promise. Now kiss me and go to sleep." I took her in my arms again and we slept, but not before blessing our lips with the goodnight kiss.

Is she really going to die? Can I convince her to start her therapies again?

The thought kept me awake for the entire night with M in my arms.

Six months have passed and not even a single day has dawned when he woke up and was not in tears. If you ask me, I believe he badly needs to see a psychiatrist, but I'm afraid to bring that up right now. Right now I'm just doing what he needs the most and what I was asked to do – be his unconditional support.

He is entering the coffee shop, with his laptop bag tucked around his right shoulder. He looks tired, depressed and preoccupied. This is not my best friend from childhood – this is a person who is broken and desolated with every living cell in his body.

"So, how was it?" I ask after he pours himself a glass of water.

"Horrendous, but better than the first day," he softly answers.

"Can you narrate it?"

"Sure."

And he starts reading.

2 February

By the time I woke her up, she already had a plate containing orchid flowers and an envelope beside her. I woke her by rolling a leaf of orchid on her face. She gradually opened her eyes and blessed my morning with her smile.

"Morning!" she mumbled.

"Morning, my love!" I wished her with a brief kiss and helped her get up. She then picked up the envelope, opened it and read the note I had written for her.

Your blue sharp almond eyes,
Having a language of their own,
Never ending their temptation, seduction,
A glance of them strong enough to make me miss a beat,
You cannot take that away from me.

She blushed as she read.

"How was it?"

"Good! For a start…"

"You smart bitch!'

"*Your* smart bitch!"

And she won this one. In the past two years, I had won almost all our outsmarting competitions. I didn't mind losing now – I could lose it all my life if it helped.

"I'm hungry now!" She cutely demanded by twitching her radiating face.

"Let me make the omelette for you," I said and stood up and saw our folks standing there.

"Good morning kids!" Dad wished enthusiastically.

"Good morning dad!" We echoed together.

"I'm going to make the breakfast for us," I voluntarily opted.

"You'll need my help in that," Mom said.

"Okay, till then I'll bathe my princess!" said Dad with a smile. They didn't leave the room before noticing the orchids and envelope with a proud smile on their face.

Mom and I headed for the kitchen. As we reached, she – as a woman, always curious about recipes – told me, "So now you can teach me the secret of your special omelettes. I've heard a lot about them." She chuckled.

"Anytime mom!" I grinned.

"What do you need?"

"Six medium peeled potatoes, one yellow onion, five eggs, two boiled eggs, chopped red peppers, two-three cups of olive oil and a pan to fry."

Within five minutes she placed everything I had asked for on the platform. I then slowly started cutting the peeled potatoes in half – trying my best not to cut them paper-thin.

"Why are you being so careful with the potatoes? We could chop them in the chopper!" Mom asked curiously.

"Well, always take care of not using the chopper for making this omelette. It will cut them too thin, which will ruin the shape and taste too." She nodded her head and started cutting the peeled onions.

After cutting the potatoes and boiled eggs adequately thin, I mixed them with onions and salted the mixture. I then picked up a non-stick frying pan, heated the olive oil on medium heat. By carefully placing the mixture of potatoes, boiled eggs and onion into the frying pan, I spread them all over the surface. I revealed the first secret to her,

"At this point, you must take care of not burning the potatoes. It will affect the taste otherwise. The oil should cover almost all the potatoes." She nodded in affirmation and I poked a piece of potato with a spatula to check if it breaks in two – it did. I signalled to mom that the potatoes were done. I then removed them from the pan with a spatula, allowing the oil to drain. After frying them, I placed the potato and onion mixture in a colander for a few minutes to allow more oil to drain. I did not forget to place a plate underneath to catch the oil, which I was about to use later.

It was now the time for my favourite part, cracking eggs. I cracked them in a large mixing bowl and beat them with a fork. I poured it in the mixture of onion, potatoes, and boiled eggs and mixed them together with a large spoon. I then picked up the smaller non-stick frying pan and let it heat on medium heat. When it started stirring, I placed the mixture into the pan and spreader it evenly. I then revealed two more secrets.

"Mom! One, do not forget to add chopped red pepper. Adding it later has its own reward. It will make the omelette a little more spicy and delicious. Two, allow the egg to cook around the edges." She smiled at my determination and only then I realised how much I was sweating. I was delighted and at the same time optimistic for my hard work to pay off.

I then carefully lifted it up to see if it was browned enough or not – it was. It was going as I had hoped. Inside of the mixture was not completely cooked and the egg was still runny. I revealed my fourth secret to her.

"Mom, after cooking one side for four minutes, make sure that the bottom is brown just as it is; realise that it is now the time to flip the side. Do it by placing a dinner plate over the frying pan and then flip it over but, not before warming it for thirty seconds." I showed her as I said. I then shaped the sides of the omelette by spatula. After five minutes of cooking, I turned off the heat. I then revealed to her my fifth secret.

"Now that we have our omelette ready and cooked, do not get excited. Keep your calm and let it sit in the pan for two-minutes," I quipped. She, by the time was impressed with my art of cooking, and patted my shoulder in appreciation.

When our princess arrived, breakfast was already waiting to go inside her ravenous mouth. Dad drove her beside me and I placed the napkin on her lap. I then picked up the butter-knife and fork, cut a slice from it and fed her.

"Mmm... This, I missed even more than you," she gagged with a blink in her magnetic blue eyes.

"Obviously, a fat omelette is better than a fat boyfriend," I simpered; she clenched her teeth with anger. I won this one. I can't let her win each one without making an effort; it was against the rule. She ate her portion slowly and peacefully until she had her stomach full. I drove her to our room where she could rest while I held her hand.

In the afternoon, Ansh came. I needed him for the part I was writing. At first knowing that I was writing our story for her astounded him. Even with the pain in his heart, he told me everything I asked him, as honestly as he could. When he read the part I wrote, he said he would come back at night to hear my narration.

True to his words, he arrived just after dinner. Dad had already prepared the guest room for him to stay. After having coconut carrot soup made by me and mom, we three headed to our room where the words written in my diary were waiting to be told. After placing my girl on her bed, I sat beside her and Ansh sat on the chair.

And I started reading.

Ansh woke up and picked his phone to check the time. It was already seven. He stood up from his bed in a hurry. Gajju was still sleeping. He tried to wake him by shaking his body.

"Wake up, bro! Only half n' hour left for the party. I don't want to miss a moment there," he said enthusiastically.

"You go Ansh! I don't want to come. I'm having a severe headache and you know I can't bear those loud speakers and DJs with this burning head of mine," he answered with partly opened eyes.

His headache problem was really irritating Ansh and had been spoiling many moments like this ever since their childhood.

"Okay then, you go to sleep, I'll bring some food for you here after the party," he said and went inside the bathroom for a shower. Unlike most hostels, they had their personal attached bathrooms and lavatories for individual rooms – the only commendable thing about the boys' hostel. Ansh took a shower, came out, and wore a white shirt and black coat with black shining trousers. Then he placed his feet into the shoes that he had polished specially for the fresher's party. Dhruv didn't move an inch all the while.

He then stepped down and took a walk to the examination hall where this party was being held. He was unstoppable; moving his legs swiftly and enthusiastically – there was nothing that could stop him – except the voice he heard.

"Excuse me, sir! Can you tell me where the examination hall is?" He heard a voice from behind. He turned around and saw a girl standing at the entrance of the girls' hostel. He looked into her eyes. No makeup, no eyeliners or mascara. Yet, she was beautiful. He could never forget the moment he saw her for the first time; miraculous hazel eyes, a cute button nose, full lips and a mouth full of straight white teeth. She wore blue jeans and black T-shirt – not any usual party clothes from any manner but were suiting perfectly on her radiating white skin. Ansh was checking her out – she too noticed it and cleared her throat.

"First year?" He started the conversation as a good guy.

"Yes, sir!" She interpreted him as a senior.

"Actually, I'm also looking for it. I'm in the first year too," Ansh lied to her, knowing that this may buy him some time with her.

"Oh! Sorry, I didn't notice you on the introduction day. So, I thought you might be from a senior batch." She uttered those words clearly, without hesitation.

Didn't notice me? Do I look that bad? Or is she just insulting me?

"Never mind, we could search for it together if you don't mind!" He offered politely, trying to make up for that.

"Okay. According to my information, it is behind the dental college," she instructed.

"Okay let's walk there." Ansh was not missing a single chance to look into her eyes. He didn't know the reason, but there was surely something enigmatic about them.

"By the way, my name is Anshul Bhatt." He introduced himself after a brief silence, but couldn't gather the courage for a handshake.

"Angel Shah…" She smiled, but didn't offer a hand either.

During that walk, they came across so many boys and girls looking at them suspiciously, Ansh and Angie were completely oblivious of the fact that walking together on the campus road of SBKS was a sign of having an affair. Ansh – compelled to keep the conversation going – asked her which school and city she belonged to. She was from Ahmedabad too. Somehow he started blushing while fantasising about their dates at various places of Ahmedabad. He started developing an irresistible attraction towards her. This walk was nevertheless heavenly for him.

"I guess we have reached, finally. Thank you for the company." She smiled again and Ansh felt a pinch of sugar. Pinch of sugar itches like any other pinch, but what makes it different is that you want it every now and then and you don't require an itch-guard for it. It was now the time for Ansh to experience it.

"Yeah, see you in class," Ansh replied, trying to match her smile, and she disappeared in the dark. Ansh couldn't enjoy the music there and was voraciously looking for her at that party but he couldn't find her. Disappointed, Ansh then headed towards the hostel, taking some food for his friend.

On the next day, he wasn't interested in what the professors were going to teach. His eyes were in search...searching for those 'Angel eyes'. He was impatiently moving his head to find her. Many of his male peers and other classmates noticed him doing that. They all started snapping at him.

'Control yourself Ansh! Your first impression in class shouldn't be of a pervert.' The thought scared Ansh.

"What is your name Mister?" The professor asked. Ansh realised he had won his attention, but like most students he still abstained himself from looking at the professor and rather looked around in disguise.

"Yes, I am talking to you boy, stand up!" Biochemistry professor stared at him in anger. Ansh, by having no other choice, finally obeyed him and stood up.

"I would have cancelled your today's attendance, but you have not been allotted roll numbers yet, so for the first and the last time I am letting you go. But these looking around things will not be tolerated in my class. You are not here to chill." His loud voice was making Ansh feel embarrassed more than ever. He was just staring at his toes.

After completing his class, he started walking, almost running towards the biochemistry practical lab.

"That was not an appropriate way to look for anything." A familiar voice came from behind. Ansh knew it was hers, and she knew he was looking for her. He didn't want to get into these confrontations, so he waffled a bit before turning around.

"I was getting bored, that's why I was looking around," Ansh was never a good self-defender.

"I thought you were searching for me." She smiled again and yet another pinch was dropped down his chest.

How the hell does she speak everything clearly without a fraction of hesitation? Doesn't she know it is embarrassing? Even if it is true!

"I wonder how are you so confident that I was looking for you?"

"Oh, it's not like that. I was just joking. Hey, I don't want to attend this practical and I am going to the canteen. Come with me if you don't mind?" she asked.

Why the hell would I?

"Oh yes, I'm also damn hungry and I was about to bunk it too." He said, trying his best not to sound desperate, but he knew he did.

"Okay, let's go." She started walking and he followed.

The professor did one favour too apart from bashing Ansh. He told them that attendance were not important till their roll numbers were allotted, but he still went to college, every day. The thing that made Ansh a regular student was 'Angel-eyes'.

M and I looked at Ansh with a smirk as I finished.

"What?" Ansh asked, irritatingly.

"You fell in love with her at first sight? Aww, how cute!" M chuckled.

"Doesn't matter now." He shrugged.

"Why?" Hearing this from a faithful lover like him astonished me. Even though I knew they were having problems when I left them, I would never think that they could drift apart.

"You missed a lot here Gajju, you were lucky," Ansh looked down.

"Like?"

"Some other time guys. You'll get all your life to bitch about my best friend after my death," she quipped. I took her hand and squeezed her palm in anger.

"Don't you ever say that again, understand?" I snapped at her.

"As if not saying this will bring me a life, c'mon Mithu! You know it's coming." I did not have an answer for her, nor did Ansh. We both remained quiet, in tears.

"It's the promise time now Mithu!" she said after a brief session of tears.

"Yes, ma'am!" I bowed at her.

"Promise me! You will complete your MBBS…no matter what."

"I'm with you on this, M!" Ansh chortled.

"Ah, you know I'm now two years behind my regular batch as I missed my final exams, but I promise." I squeezed her palm again, but this time, softly, passionately. Ansh then headed for the guest room and we spent the night in each other's arms.

After having an exhausting sweat session of aerobics, I'm sitting on the sofa opposite the reception table while he is still on the treadmill. He needs to get fitter and better. That's another promise he'll have to keep and I'm doing my job – being with him whenever and wherever he needs. After fifteen minutes, I see him coming out, sweating. Day by day, it is getting hard for me to desist myself from desiring him. As I see him more – I want him more. I won't lie to you about the warmth I feel when he is around. Whenever I think of him, I'm completely smitten by him. And he too is…I know that. Not as much as he used to, but he is.

"How was it?" He softly asks.

"Good, but not better than yours," I say with a wink, complementing his efforts.

"Aerobics and Cardio are the flip side of the same coin. They cannot be compared."

"But seems like cardio is more rewarding," I continue appreciating him – deservingly so.

"Good to hear that."

"Dhruv, you don't have to be so formal with me, you know that," I say with a frown.

"Let's not get there now. Tell me, do you want to hear further?" He says distracting my thoughts successfully.

"I'm not offering you any choice on that, you promised me, remember?"I snap at him.

"I know ma'am, all I'm trying to say is that we are not alone today."

"Then?"

"Ansh, Angie, Shilpan, Aakash, Harsh, Rishi, all are waiting for you." I literally jump as I hear that. Only I know how long I have waited for this moment to come.

"Finally!" I shrug, in joy of course.

"Yep, finally!" He smiles as we head towards his car.

He takes me to Ansh's home where everyone is present already. He introduces me to everyone, and they all greet me cordially. Within five minutes, I gel with them as if I have known them for years. Ansh, who once was finding it hard to get along with me, was smiling and singing with them: "Don't lose her again bro!" That brings a shy smile on my face. I hug Angie as I meet her – remembering something we both have lost.

"How are you bro?" Dhruv asks after introducing me to Rishi.

"Better than you, Dhruv!" He muzzles and Dhruv smiles.

"I'm sure you are." He coyly replies.

He then introduces me to Aakash, Shilpan and Harsh. They all are happy to see us together, finally. After having a long session of chattering, we all are finally silent and waiting for him to start. After reassuring our attention towards him, he pulls out his Mac.

And he starts reading.

3 February

Ansh took the initiative of being my regular supplier for orchids, and in return I allowed his presence when I read to M. I asked for her permission and she, without any reservation, agreed on this. In return, she took a promise from Ansh. Just one promise from Ansh and one every day from me? That was quite unfair. Still, I did not have any objection, as I liked those promises; they weren't hard, at least not till then. She opened the envelope after kissing the orchids.

Your always ready to turn red nose, ears,
Your always blushing and giggling cheeks,
Your always coming in a way to save you on the crucial moments – hair,
You cannot take that away from me.

Just as I sensed this coming, her nose and ears turned red in giggles. By expanding her arms, she ordered me to embrace her. I took her in my arms and gave her a passionate morning kiss. Just then, her folks entered.

"Oh oh…I should've knocked," Dad shrugged and they both went out. We laughed and informed them to come in.

"We should learn to knock before coming in." Mom quipped.

"I don't believe it was unintentional," M retorted.

"You mother-daughter are impossible!" Dad sighed.

"And you father-son, so easy." She winked, triggered tears to fall from mom's eyes. I could contemplate that they were the tears of joy. I too was having the time of my life with my new family. I managed to call my own parents once a day. They were concerned about where I was but I strictly asked them not to track me, nor ask anything till I get back. A new optimist and a sense of confidence in my voice were playing an agonist too.

It was now the time to make omelettes. Ansh was already in the kitchen preparing everything to assist me. Mom knew he was the best guy to assist me as he was my regular assistant back in Baroda. I tried to have a conversation with him to coax out what they were hiding, but in vain.

"Are you going to tell me now?"

"No Gajju! Please."

"Why Ansh? What is it?"

"You are not ready, buddy! Besides, M has given me strict instructions not to tell you anything."

So she was the one who was behind it. M, I hate you for some things. Just as I love you for most others.

"Okay, I won't push you then. But you love her, admit it."

"It will not make any difference."

"It will. You will be ensured."

"I'm ensured Gajju! Let me tell you what I feel. I still am in love with Angie, madly, and that's why it pains more. But if I keep thinking about that now, I'll screw my final year which I don't want to. I want to get through, at least for my parents' sake. Now do you need any more answers?"

"No, I got it."I said with a smile, patted his back to calm him. I didn't intend the conversation to go this belligerent.

In the afternoon when she was asleep, Ansh and I were together, writing the next part, which undoubtedly was the craziest day of our life. So we both knew that night was going to bring so much fun. M too sensed it when she woke up and was swift in finishing her dinner soup along with the salad, which Ansh had brought from my house. I was having food cooked by my mother after seven months and it never tasted more delicious. After having dinner, we three gathered in our room.

I opened the diary and started reading,

Ansh opened his eyes when he felt the touch of green grass tickling inside his ear and the cold breeze of the morning playing with his hair. He knew this wasn't the feeling he got every morning. He moved his eyes and realized,

'Bloody hell!' He shrugged.

He lay in the goalpost of the football ground and his head was spinning with excruciating pain. He anxiously reached inside his pockets to take out his phone, but they were empty.

'How the hell did I arrive here? Where are my friends?' These were some of the questions which ran in his mind, but the most important part was missing. 'What happened last night?'

He stood up and started running towards the hostel. When he was passing through the cricket ground, he saw someone lying flat on the pitch. He got closer, and feared since the figure was appearing like Dhruv. He took a close look and found his ideas turning into reality – he was right.

"What the hell man!!" Ansh took a big gasp before reaching close to his friend.

"Gajju!" Ansh yelled and shook his body.

"Ansh?" Dhruv said with groggy eyes.

"What the hell are you doing here?"

"Shut the fuck up Ansh, what happened?" He asked appraising his obliteration.

"Dude look around, you are lying in the middle of the cricket ground." He stood up with Ansh's support and looked around.

"O gosh, my head…" He screamed and placed his hand over his head.

"I think it's because of a hangover Gajju!"

"Don't get filmy Ansh."

"Oh really? I found myself in football ground and you here. What does it mean? Do you remember what happened last night?" Behind Ansh's sarcasm, there was a hope.

"No, I think… results came out in the evening, I passed with grace and we decided to party, trying booze for the first time… and…"

"Exactly! Our result, party and then, blank. I remember the same and by knowing the fact that we are college students and still inside the campus, this is even worse than the movies," Dhruv stood pale, and was as clueless as Ansh was.

"Now move your ass and let's go to the hostel. I wish no one has seen us," Ansh angrily said, because it was Dhruv's idea to include alcohol and he had pestered Ansh to drink. When they were walking through the campus road, seeing their biggest fear turning real, they saw every person – no matter boy or girl – laughing at them. They were having the same feeling as a male escort would have, watching his family when his true identity is revealed.

"Dude, some real shit happened last night," Gajju muttered.

"As I feared, Gajju!"

When they were about to reach the hostel, they saw Shilpan coming from a sideway. He was all wet – as if he was all out in the rain and they all knew it hadn't rained last night.

"Just tell us where you found yourself?" Gajju asked, cutting off all unnecessary points.

"In the water tank," Shilpan dismayed.

"What????? In the water tank??? Any memory?" Ansh asked astonished.

"Our result came, and…"

"Got it, no need to say more. We both are stuck at that part only." Gajju shrugged in disappointment.

As they entered inside, they saw thrashed TVs, wardrobes, wooden beds, steel and plastic chairs in the centre hall which was also their basketball court.

"I'm afraid if we have to do anything with this, Gajju!" Shilpan murmured.

'*If he is right, then we are totally fucked up,*' Ansh thought.

"I'm sorry Shilpan, but I think we have," Dhruv had prepared himself for every worst scenario.

"I'll kill you, bastard!" Ansh gave him a shot of disdain. Dhruv frowned in return.

They went to the third floor and saw Aakash standing in the lobby.

"Finally, we will get to know what happened!" Gajju said enthusiastically. The only part they remembered was that Aakash had refused to drink. Dhruv got closer to embrace him, but before he could go any closer, Aakash slapped him. It was so tight that even a self-proclaimed tough guy like Dhruv went numb for a while.

"What happened man?" Shilpan blurted in anger.

"Ask him! What have you guys done?" Aakash growled, exceeding his anger.

"Sorry Aakash, but the three of us doesn't remember a single thing about what happened," Ansh said trying to calm him.

"Drunk bastards! See for yourself what you have done," Aakash said, pointing towards the trashes.

"You mean, we did all this?" Shilpan asked in scepticism.

"Every single thing – along with all the other boys in the hostel. You instigated them to do this stuff – especially you," he said and snapped at Dhruv who was still standing with his hand on his cheek.

"But why are you so angry with me man?" Dhruv asked, finally.

"Come with me," he said and took us to his room; without uttering a word, they followed. As they entered, they saw a broken chair with a white thick rope near the bed.

"See this broken chair and rope? When you four went crazy, I tried to stop you, but this bastard tied me with these ropes and everything which occurred after that is history." Everyone was struggling to restrain their laughter, but no one could hide a smile.

"Sorry bro!" Gajju said with a smirk.

"Fuck you asshole! I couldn't sleep all night because of you motherfuckers!" Fuming Aakash groaned.

"But where is everyone else?" Shilpan came to our rescue to change the topic.

"Most of them have left the hostel and others are in their respective rooms."

"Why are you here then?" Dhruv asked. Aakash stared at him.

"Because of you fuckers! Where the hell have you been?"

"I don't know! The only thing I remember is that when I woke up, I found myself in the football net and Gajju on the cricket pitch," Ansh joined.

"And I woke up in the central water tank. I opened my eyes when they started filling the empty tank," Shilpan muttered.

"What? Water tank? How the hell did you all reach there?" Aakash asked, completely astonished by the answers.

"By the way, where is Harsh? Did he come here?" Shilpan looked around, being the first one to notice his absence.

"I thought he was with you guys!" Aakash replied.

"No man. He was not with us. But where the hell is he?"Ansh almost screamed in worry.

"Don't panic guys, just call him," Dhruv suggested.

"How smart Gajju! But you all smartly dropped your phones in this drawer last night," Aakash said, pulled out their phones from the drawer and gave them back.

Ansh looked at the screen and there were about thirty missed calls from Angie. He called her back.

"Thank god you finally called!"

"Angie, last night...."

"I know. Actually the whole campus knows."

"What? How?"

"You don't remember what you have done?"

"Sorry to say Angie, but no. I just found myself in the football ground and that's all I know."

"Ansh, you..."

"You can save your miff for later, Angie! Right now help us find Harsh if you can. He is missing."

"Just call him!"

"He is the missing one Angie, not his phone."

"Shit. Okay, I'll call you if I get to know anything."

"Okay bye!"

Ansh ended his call and turned around and saw Shilpan waiting for him.

"Got any information, Ansh?" Shilpan asked in worry.

"No! I think this time, it went over the head Shilpan!" Ansh said with consternation.

"Yeah! But right now we should focus on finding Harsh," Shilpan said, trying his best to stay optimistic.

They started their quest, knowing that it was necessary to find him before the warden and other officials would show up. They had about thirty minutes. They all washed their faces, changed their clothes, gargled with Listerine and went out.

They all were on a conference call, mission objective, "Find HARSH BHAVSAR."

"Gajju, anything on ground floor?"

"Negative. Just trashes allegedly created by us."

"Shilpan, on first floor?"

"Negative."

"Aakash, second floor?"

"Negative."

"Ansh, Third floor?"

"Negative – just seeing every one laughing at me."

"Same here dude!"

"I think we rocked it last night, what say Aakash?"

"Fuck you, Gajju!"

"Come and do it by yourself."

"Stop this cat fight guys and concentrate on finding him."

"Guys, I have to disconnect. Angie's call is intervening continuously. I think she has got something," Ansh disconnected himself from the conference call and called her.

"Hello!"

"Ansh, I've found him."

"Where?"

"At the north outer lobby of the second floor."

"What? In the girls' hostel?"

"Yeah."

"Man! Let me inform others. Angie, just keep an eye on him."

"Okay."

Ansh then called Aakash, who seemed the most responsible guy at that time.

"Dude, I've got some good news and some bad."

"Could that bad be worse than what we have right now?"

"Indeed."

"Then don't tell me Ansh."

"Harsh is on the second floor."

"That's great yaar! But I'm on the second floor and I can't find him."

"Because he is on the second floor of the girls' hostel."

Disconnected.

'*Responsible guy my ass!*' Ansh shrugged.

After two minutes, Dhruv called him.

"Ansh, is it true?"

"Yes, Gajju! Angie just found him there."

"Okay then you go there, I'm on my way."

Within five minutes, they all gathered. Angie was standing on the second floor where harsh was lying.

"Just wake him Angie," Ansh signalled and she followed.

Within two minutes, he looked down with his unsteady eyes and looked as ambivalent as the rest of them were when they had woken up.

"Dude, what are you doing upstairs?" Aakash shouted.

"No point in asking that Aakash!" Shilpan said.

"What happened guys? How the hell did I get here?" Harsh said, clearly baffled.

"We are yet to find out, dude. Were you sober when you arrived here?" Dhruv asked.

"Not even in my dreams, Dhruv!" he answered.

"Then how did you climb up asshole?" Aakash yelled. Ansh calmed him by signalling Angie's presence there.

Before they could come up with a better idea, Dhruv started climbing through edges and jumped onto the first floor. In an attempt of being spider-man – well he didn't do it in the signature spider-man way – he surely did it in a monkey way.

"Oh shit! Warden is coming. Gajju, Harsh hide," Shilpan yelled as he saw the warden coming.

"Dude, we can get rusticated if he finds Gajju and Harsh," Aakash muttered.

"Shut up man! Be positive. None of this is going to happen." Ansh tried to calm everyone, but somewhere inside, he knew that optimism was not his forte.

"What are you doing here, boys? Stalking girls?" Warden suspiciously asked.

"No, sir! I called my friend to give me some notes," Ansh said taking the charge.

"So where is she? And why are you not waiting for her outside the front gate?" Warden asked apprising that he wasn't dumb at all.

They all looked up, but no one was there. Ansh tried to call her again, but got no response!

'No man she cannot leave me here like this. She has to help us. Only she can.' Ansh thought.

"She will be coming soon sir!" Ansh confidently said.

"That won't be needed," he said and took out his phone.

"Hello, girls' hostel? Have a look at all floors of north wings, and then report to me." His call scared them as he had already sensed something fishy by their hesitation and unnecessary fear.

"Who scathed all this college property?" He asked with suspicious eyes.

"We don't know, sir!" Shilpan answered.

"As expected. Everyone in the hostel is saying that. Then who did this? Ghosts? There are reports of some drunken students shouting all night and sleeping on the grounds. If any one of you knows anything about them, I warn you, speak up." He said in fury; that was the best thing about their hostel life, unity. No one took even a single name.

'If any official didn't see us there, we are saved.' Ansh sighed.

They all stood pale, trying their best to avoid any more conversations and only then they saw Dhruv and Harsh coming out from the front gate of the girls' hostel along with female wardens.

'Fuck man, what are you guys doing? Are you out of your mind?' Aakash shuddered.

They all started sweating and the heat was merely playing any part in that perspiration. They came closer and joined the rest.

"I've called my father. He is on his way. My friends are innocent; please let them go, sir!" Dhruv said.

"You are not the one to decide that; the committee will decide. Let your father come. Till then you all are prohibited from leaving the hostel and campus. Follow us to my cabin," he said and started walking; they followed him without sharing a word.

They were sitting outside the warden's office, waiting for Mr. Kaushik Gajjar, Dhruv's father.

"Should we inform our parents too?" Shilpan asked, being concerned.

"Not needed bro. Let my dad come, he will handle everything for everyone," Gajju confidently answered.

"I hope he does, because you are the real culprit, not us," snapped still agitated Aakash.

"Stop picking on him man! Bash me instead, we all are here because of me and I don't even remember how I got up there," Harsh said, lifting his hand to his brow and rubbing his sweating forehead.

"None of us do buddy," Gajju, who managed to keep himself composed, said.

"I do," said Aakash.

"What?" Harsh asked in disguise.

"Ansh found himself in the football net. Gajju on the cricket pitch and I found myself inside the central water trunk as I woke up. None of us remember how we got there," Shilpan answered, taking a deep audible sigh.

"Fucking hell!" Blurted dumbstruck Harsh.

"Want to see something more interesting?" Gajju simpered.

"What?"

"Have a look at the basketball court!" Harsh stood up and walked there.

"Don't tell me we did all this." His eyes went wide open like saucers.

"All you fuckers were involved," Aakash said.

"Except you fatty! Sorry to restrain you from joining the party," Gajju winked.

"Gajju, but why did you come out? I was calling Angie and she could've saved us," Ansh intervened, obviously to avoid their collision.

"I know Ansh! Even Angie offered us to hide in her room, but what after that? The hostel was already on high alert and if anyone would have caught me, Harsh and Angie together, then you can imagine how much trouble it could bring for her. So I sent her back and told her not to respond to you at the moment. I would never risk any girl's reputation to save my ass, and Angie? She is my beloved 'Bhabhijan', so how could I?" He chuckled. Ansh couldn't manage to respond, however, he wanted Dhruv to keep teasing him, and somehow Dhruv knew it too.

"But why did you call your father this soon? I mean you played a safe side for us, but you can get rusticated for this. We should have faced the consequences together, not you alone," Shilpan said apprising his faith in team work.

"Let him come. You will understand why I called him. He will surely have a word with me, admonish me for not getting involved again, but he will save us for sure. And my passing grades will play agonists in this too," Gajju's faith in his father was playing the role of Glucon-D for the rest.

Meanwhile, Ansh saw Mr. Gajjar coming and poked Dhruv. Dhruv suddenly changed his position and sat quietly – staring at his toes. He saw Ansh and smiled. He too greeted him with his eyes. He ignored Dhruv. As the warden saw him through the glass, he came out to greet him; they shook hands and went inside.

After about ten minutes, the warden came out and asked Ansh to come inside alone and he followed.

"So tell me Ansh, what happened? What was Dhruv doing in the girls' hostel?" Mr. Kaushik asked.

'How do I know uncle! I don't even know what I was doing on the football ground.' Ansh thought, but he knew this answer of him would confirm their involvement in property loss.

"There was a bet between them uncle, for who can climb it! They had no intention to harm any girl, sir!" He looked at the warden and he was smiling too, along with Mr. Gajjar. Ansh too knew that there was no way on earth they would have believed him.

"I told you, sir! This must be one of his mischiefs. He has been mischievous from childhood. Besides, he means no harm to anyone ever. You can ask Ansh. He is Dhruv's friend since the day they both marked their first step in school," Mr. Gajjar defended his son's actions.

'Are they convinced? Seriously? No way, I bet I would find uncle's cheque-book in his pocket.'

"But stepping into the girls' hostel without permission is a criminal offence, Mr. Gajjar!" the warden said. Ansh thought to increase the amount of his argument.

"Well, I think that should be settled sir! You want me to call our dean and talk about this? At last he is going to be the one to take a final decision." Then Ansh began to understand why Gajju called his father. Few more cheques and Dhruv might get a room inside the girls' hostel. Well, he wouldn't mind joining him there. No one would.

"It is okay, Mr. Gajjar, but there is one problem. I can save them from legal actions, but your son will have to leave the hostel," Warden said.

Kaushik uncle looked at Ansh and smiled.

'Yes, it worked uncle. Bingo! No more cheques!'

"That won't be a problem sir! I already have an unused property in Vadodara City, which is just ten kilometres away from here. They will shift there, and I'm sure that property damage you are talking about, they are not involved in that." Ansh lifted his gaze at the warden; he wasn't happy, wasn't even smiling. He was sure that warden wasn't happy with what he had to get settled with; lack of evidence, thank you.

Three of them came out. All friends were looking at Ansh with a big question mark expression. He just had to smile and wink; it was enough for them to understand they all could sigh in relief.

"Dhruv and Harsh, you will have to write an apology letter for getting MISPLACED in the girls' hostel," the warden said.

"And you and Ansh are going to shift to our house in the city. Your friends can also join you there if they want. Ansh, don't worry, I'll inform your parents about it," Mr. Gajjar said.

"Yes, uncle!" He meekly replied.

"And I'm expecting you two at the parking lot. I want to have a word with you two." He demanded and walked out.

"Dude, your dad is really cool! He settled everything in less than thirty minutes!" Shilpan said in joy.

"You have seen only one side of him bro! Now I'm going to face another." He was right, so right. As they walked to the parking lot, they saw him standing outside his car waiting for them. His driver was sitting inside.

"First of all, congratulations to you both for the result!" He was calm. It was the same silence that calms everything before the tornado; the real tornado was waiting to explode.

"Thanks uncle!" Ansh said and he smiled.

"Thanks dad!" Gajju said and he didn't respond.

"Just answer my question. Are you responsible for that property damage? And I'm sure you have a good reason to convince my faith in you why you went in girls' hostel," he said.

"May be dad," he replied looking down.

'Man! Are you nuts? What the fuck do you want to be? An ideal son?'

"What do you mean by may be?" Mr. Gajjar asked with a confused and angry look. They were sweating by that time and this time too, the heat was merely playing a minor role.

"Dad, when results came out, we decided to party, and alcohol was also included in it for the first time. After that what happened is still an enigma. I climbed there because my friend was there and no one knows how he reached there." He answered.

Mr. Gajjar looked at Ansh, this time not smiling. He knew Dhruv was going to get the piece of his meat. Ansh was thinking about intervening, but before he could come up with something, SLAP!!! A father slapped his son tightly; this was the second time Dhruv was getting slapped on the same day.

"Ansh, in the past, when he used to get into things like these, you were the one who always pulled him out. But I guess this time you also got carried away with him!!" He was right. Ansh looked down.

Just don't slap me man! I'm not your son. Even my father doesn't slap.'

"Promise me Dhruv! That this is the last time I'm pulling you out of this mess."

"Promise dad," Dhruv said.

"Now, you see that new white Volkswagen Vento?" He asked, pointing towards a new white car.

"Yes, dad!" Dhruv said, barely glanced at it.

"This is for you, as I promised. You passed the first year with grace marks but you passed, so here it is." Dhruv got his energy back in no time and hugged Mr.Gajjar in joy. Ansh was just witnessing a great father-son equation.

"Listen, drive responsibly. When you are holding the steering wheel in your hand, you don't hold just your life, but you hold the lives of all other people who care for you. If you over speed it and something occurs, it affects their lives more than yours," Mr.Gajjar instructed, handed the keys to Gajju and sat in his car.

After he went, they started walking towards the hostel.

"Dude you almost got us killed," Ansh said.

"No buddy, it was an obligation for me to tell him the truth. If you remember a few years back, when I got in some serious trouble, I lied to him, which led me into more trouble. Then he took a promise from me that I won't tell a lie whenever I would get in any trouble. That's why…"

After hearing this short satire of his, they turned to the hostel and saw their three friends coming.

"Dude, really you're going to leave the hostel?" Shilpan asked.

"Yup, but no need to worry! Poor warden has done us a favour. Now we can have more fun. At both the places," Dhruv said and winked.

"You can fuck yourself anywhere Gajju. Just give me the key. I saw you got a new ride," Aakash demanded.

"Ya great ride Gajju! I'm getting the same, but in blue colour," Shilpan enthusiastically said to quote the line, *'Boys and cars, a deadly combination.'*

"So, two places, two cars and five wolves. Seems like this town will go on fire," Harsh simpered.

But one thing is still and will remain a mystery forever.

What the hell happened that night? And how did they end up waking up in those places?

The three of us broke into laughter as I finished. This was the memory of a lifetime. Though I got rusticated from the hostel, I did not regret it. Well, I regret the trouble I gave to my father because of that, but keeping that apart, it was a hell lot of fun.

"And you guys still don't know what happened that night?" M asked.

"No, everyone tried to remember what might have happened, but none of us do," I answered.

"Aakash does." Ansh winked and we guffawed again.

Ansh was feeling sleepy so he stood up and went out. M and I chattered about the event for a while until she had all her answers. Just before we went to sleep, she said, "Mithu, it's promise time."

"Yes, ma'am!" I said with obeisance.

"Promise me! You'll be the string which will hold your family and friends together."

"Promise, my love!" I accepted without any reservation.

Few days have passed and yet I feel like it happened an hour ago, the reunion where I met his…our friends. We laughed together, we ate together and somewhere down the line, without letting each other know, we cried together. They all couldn't stop guffawing when Dhruv narrated the hangover part. Everyone had come with their own theory of what might've happened. Aakash, who knew more than anyone else, was surprisingly sitting quietly with a smile on his face. There was an awkward silence when Dhruv narrated the part where he tied him with that rope. I could see their hidden smirk behind the silence.

He comes with a smile on his face, opens the door and sits inside his car.

"Where to?" I ask without attempting to hide my cheer.

"My secret place…" I snap at him, dumbstruck by the answer.

"What? You are not kidding right?" I ask in skepticism.

"No, let's go." I hug him in joy as soon as I hear it.

He drives me to the riverfront. It is better now, only for people. He liked it more when it did not have any railings so that he could just sit for hours and let his feet relax and to get massaged naturally and obviously – to think about me. It is now more clean, beautiful and near perfect, but not for him. I can see it in his eyes.

"Thank you for bringing me here," I say and hold his hand. Although it is not his secret place anymore, but he still loves it here.

"Let's start then! You will love today's part." He chuckles.

"Then what are you waiting for?" I coyly answer, knowing that today he might introduce me to you all.

And he starts reading.

My name is Nirali Shah. I'm his first love...even before M, but not anymore. He is the first and last person I fell in love with, and even with all his pain, anguish and frustration, he cannot take that away from me.

4 February

On that day, there were two different orchids, the usual purple ones and the second, having a stripe of white. Orchids are odourless but she used to smell it every day and when I asked her why she was doing this, she said that she could feel my presence in them. I then used to muzzle that she could feel me more by giving me a passionate kiss and she – as if waiting for me to say that – would lean towards me to give that passionate morning kiss. I then used to run my fingers across her waist, which could ignite her passion even higher. Although we'd been in a relationship for the past two years, we did not get intimate with each other completely, but we surely ascertained many hidden secrets about us. The fourth note along with the flowers said,

> *Your waist, always a favourite for my fingers to run across,*
> *Your most sensitive navel and flat belly,*
> *A pinch on it provokes you to embrace me in your arms,*
> *You cannot take that away from me.*

She looked away, blushed and poked me to give her another kiss. She asked me to get my hands off her waist, but I knew what her heart was echoing – it was commanding me to make my grip even tighter, my love broke into moans with every kiss.

I was making breakfast with Ansh while M was playing games on my iPhone in our room. There was an awkward silence between us, and we both knew why.

"She is coming today Ansh!"

"I don't care Gajju!"

"Yes, you do, accept it."

"Will you stop her from coming if I say I do?"

"No, you know buddy, I need her for the part I'm writing."

"No, you don't! I have told you everything and there is nothing more she can spice you up with, even with her most amazing lies."

"I know you told me everything from your side but remember, there are always three sides of any story – their version, your version and the truth. And my job is to write the truth for my girl."

I winked and patted his back. He stood still without uttering a word. After all, it was about M.

In the afternoon after lunch, my blue-eyed girl and I were sitting on the bed when Angie knocked the door.

"Hello! Hope I'm not causing any disturbance."

"No ma'am, you are more than welcome. By the way Angie, someone is getting older," I quipped with a wink.

"And someone is getting fatter," she retorted.

"By the way, Ansh is outside, you met him?"

Before my girl could speak anything, she replied, "I'm getting engaged Dhruv!" she mumbled.

My eyebrows went up in shock. "What?" I knew they were hiding something, but I surely didn't expect this.

"What? How?" I arched my brows at her.

"I told you Gajju, you missed many things here, you were lucky,"Ansh came inside and sat beside me. Angie was quietly looking down.

"Stop it guys! This is not the time to speak about it and if you want to fight, do it outside. I'm having my last dates with my boyfriend and I won't let you guys spoil it," M admonished. Everyone had to obey her; we were quiet in no time. That afternoon when my girl went to sleep, I heard Angie's version of the story and penned it down with all my heart and of course, some old faded memories.

On that day, we had a quiet dinner, having Ansh and Angie with us. I was regretting why I left them when they needed me the most, but there was no way on earth I could say it. She was already blaming herself for that. We four were sitting in our room waiting for me to start.

And so I started reading.

After enjoying their dinner till late in the night, the boys were in a hurry to drop Angie at the girls' hostel. On the way, they saw a girl sitting on the sideway bench. Her hands covered her eyes and it appeared as if she was crying. Angie told Dhruv to stop the car and he obeyed.

"M? What's she doing here?" Angie blurted.

"Who's she?" Ansh asked.

"M*****. Our immediate junior, she is my friend, but what's she doing here?"

"Another blonde without a brain, crying on the road. How dumb!" Dhruv said casually, and Angie snapped at him with anger, stepping out and walking towards her.

"Hey M, what's the matter? Why are you sitting here alone? And why are you crying?" Angie asked tapping her back.

"Hi Angel! Don't you know our hostel gate closes at ten? It's already ten now! I'm trying to find an auto since an hour, but can't find any, because of the strike," she said in sobs.

Ansh and Dhruv were standing as rocks, letting Angie handle her. This was the first time when Dhruv saw M. Appearing as another blonde without brain, but there was something different about her, which was persistent in catching Dhruv's attention – her natural blue eyes. Dhruv could not keep himself away from looking at them.

"I know dear, but we do not have any other choice, do we?" Angie stood beside her and they heard her sobs too.

'Oh c'mon Angie, what's this? You were having fun a few minutes back. Remember?' The thoughts echoed inside of Ansh's mind.

For a minute or two, no one spoke. M was weeping on Angie's arms and Angie too was trying hard to match her tears, like they were competing with each other for who can shed more tears?

"There is one option. Why don't you stay at my house?" Dhruv uttered.

Ansh glanced at him with a big question mark. There was a deep silence. Both girls were looking at them with disarray.

"Are you sure there won't be any problem?" Angie asked. There was a bit of affirmation in her voice, which amused them, especially Ansh.

"I think so, because tomorrow is Sunday so no one will notice your absence tonight as most Ahmedabadi students will be out too," Dhruv said.

'Great going dude!' mumbled Ansh.

They both looked at each other. M already had stopped crying and by taking a note of their body language, guys knew that they were almost ready.

"M, if you don't have any problem..." Angie didn't finish her words and left the final call to M.

"It's okay if you are with me," M said and gave her affirmation.

"Okay, then let's go!" Dhruv swiftly moved, by giving them no further chance to rethink.

They reached Dhruv's house. Dhruv signalled Ansh about the mess they had to clean before they could take the girls inside.

"You two just wait here in the car, Ansh and I are going inside to sweep up a little," Dhruv said.

"Stop! It's okay dear. I know how you guys are and I actually want to see boys' room. How bad can you guys make it!" Angie smirked.

"But..." Ansh was saying when Dhruv interrupted.

"It's okay Ansh, she wants to see guys' room, so let's show it to her," Dhruv smiled back.

They went inside, and the boys led them to their room. Their dirty boxers and undergarments were flooded on the floor, smelling like rotten fruits.

"Anything more you want to see my dear?" Dhruv simpered.

"Very funny, want any help in cleaning this mess?" Angie offered.

"That's really sweet of you, but not needed. You girls go downstairs and sit in the dining room. We will join you in a while." They went downstairs and the boys joined them after mopping the floor and making their room less terrible.

"What will we do now?" Angie asked.

"Let's play a game. Spin the bottle."

Girls agreed in an instant; they always reserve a soft corner for these types of games.

"M, if you don't have any problem," Dhruv asked for assurance.

"No, it's okay. You guys have done so much for me that I can't find enough words to thank you. So I'm fine with whatever you decide," she meekly replied.

"No need to be formal dear. You know we would never let you sit there alone," Angie consoled her.

"If you want to play this, then only participate. Otherwise, it's fine. No one is pushing you," Dhruv firmly said.

'Why is this fucker being so polite today?' Ansh wondered.

"No, I'm fine with it. Let's play," M said, giving her assurance with a smile. Boys wondered, who would say that these girls were weeping just an hour ago?

Gajju went upstairs and brought an empty bottle of vodka. Angie snapped at Ansh with anger.

"This doesn't belong to me, take a troll at him," Ansh gave his rational explanation.

"I found this one only, hope you two are fine with it," Dhruv said.

"It's okay. We don't have any problem," Girls said unanimously.

"But you guys better stay away from these. I don't need to remind you how good you are with them," Angie chuckled.

"Objection sustained," Dhruv retorted with a wink.

'That's my girl you motherfucker!' Ansh echoed in his mind.

Then M spun the bottle, and the cap pointed towards Dhruv.

"Who was the first girl in your life?" She asked.

"Nirali…" Dhruv said and paused, "Nirali Shah."

"Tell us more about her," Angie demanded.

"Sorry, one question at a time," Dhruv muzzled and spun the bottle, and the cap then pointed at M.

"What is your checklist when you find a guy to date?" Dhruv asked.

"Ahmm, none actually; who will touch the chords of my heart, will be my special one," she answered politely.

"And how many special ones have touched those strings till now?" Dhruv asked without reservation.

"Sorry…one question at a time," she retorted with a smirk and spun the bottle. Cap pointed at Angie and bottom at Dhruv.

"Tell us the biggest lie of your life which you don't regret," he asked.

She clenched her teeth and showed him a punch. Dhruv responded with a wink and threw a kiss. Ansh realised it had to do something with him.

She turned to Ansh, "Remember, I asked you about the way to examination hall?" He nodded. "I lied, I knew the way."

"Why?" Ansh blurted.

"Rules are rules, my friend! One question at a time," Dhruv came to her rescue. Ansh saw Angie giving Gajju a shot of gratitude and spun the bottle. It pointed at M again with the bottom towards Ansh.

"Tell me how many guys have touched those strings?" Dhruv desperately asked before Ansh could say something, she too noticed it and smiled generously.

"None, really none! They are fully untouched, reserved for someone special," she answered with a certain pride in her voice.

"There is nothing in that to be proud of," Dhruv chortled.

"I know. Don't worry, I'm not one of those stereotypes. It's just that I never found someone who could really touch them. To be honest, I really wanted to, but I never got one," she explained and spun the bottle. Cap pointed at Dhruv again. Ansh was enjoying everyone's confessions and was completely fine by not getting that cap pointed towards him.

"Tell us more about her," M demanded. Her extra attention towards Dhruv got Ansh and Angie's eyes suspicious.

"We used to sit together in class and were best of friends. I had interacted with many girls in my life but no one got my attention as much as she did," Dhruv said.

"Really? No one?" Angie chuckled, with her eyes arched at M.

"And? You guys were dating?" M asked, paying no attention to Angie.

"No no, never! But I liked her – as a friend, and as a great companion. Apart from Ansh, she was the only one with whom I could share anything…and I mean anything!"

"And there was a time when she was even more important than me," Ansh shrugged.

"She was your friend too?" Angie asked.

"No, she wasn't. Ansh didn't like her. He was very possessive about me then." He chuckled.

"Ya right, but that was childhood. You know how much effort I put for your patch up when she was gone," Ansh retorted with a grin.

"Where did she go?" Asked M.

"She went into designing and I was sent here. So after that, I never heard from her," Dhruv answered and everyone saw a smile on M's face.

They kept spinning the bottle for about an hour till they started getting bored.

"What do we do now? Should we go to sleep?" Angie asked.

"Sure, if you want to. You are the owner of your time," Dhruv said, who was at his most polite mood.

"You got any better idea?" M's eye lit up.

"Let me advise you one thing M, never ever ask or consider Gajju's ideas," Ansh chuckled. Angie too nodded her head, how could she forget that he almost got them rusticated?

"He is right M, because I have an idea in my mind, which may seem crazy to you all," Dhruv exploited.

"We are all ears," quipped Angie.

"Why don't we go out for a coffee or something?"

"For the first time, I'm not finding your suggestion crazy," Angie smirked.

"Because I'm not finished yet," Dhruv paused.

"Then?"

"At my favourite restaurant – Cafe piano!" Dhruv unveiled his yet another crazy desire.

"What? Dude, are you mad? You want to travel 120 km for just a coffee and that too with girls at night?"Ansh grumbled.

"I told you that you will find it crazy, but tell me guys, do you want to?"Dhruv tossed his coin again. Both the girls looked at each other, waiting for the other person to say something.

"Of course, I don't want to," Ansh growled, hoping that girls would join him soon, but to his surprise, they didn't respond.

"I want to,"blasted Angie.

She then looked at M, who was still pale.

"I don't mind!" To Ansh's surprise, she responded positively too. Then Dhruv – along with both girls – snapped at Ansh.

"Whyyyyyy…would I mind then?"A sudden change in his opinion made everyone laugh.

"Okay then, let's ride." Dhruv said enthusiastically. Within the next five minutes they were in the car and on their way to Ahmedabad. Ahmedabad-Baroda expressway never seemed better for them – less traffic, smoother roads and their favourite music. Hardly anyone spoke a word throughout the journey and yet, it was blissful. Dhruv – always a faithful lover of road trips – had his own collection of old and new songs prepared. Most of them were soft, enchanting and romantic songs which Dhruv considered best for the road trips. He – from all the experiences of both night drives and long drives – believed that loud music bores you within one hour and will turn your blissful ride into a lousy and exhausting one. Knowing that there were girls on their backseats, Dhruv had taken care that no matter how much the smooth roads of the expressway would seduce him to over speed, he never would. As soon as they reached Ahmedabad, they recognised that it was Saturday night and patrolling on Saturday nights is always high. But Dhruv, less concerned about the police, knew another way where there would be no patrolling even if they impose curfew. To everyone's surprise, he was true to his words. He led them to TGB-Cafe Piano in no time, without any interruptions. As they both were loyal customers there and since for the first time they had girls with them, everyone from the gatekeepers to the waiters was treating them with more enthusiasm. More so, they were expecting less trouble. Three hours passed like a couple of minutes, with espresso shots, Pasta arrabiata and Devils on horseback. It was already five in the morning when they left TGB. This was Ansh's longest night-out and that too with the girl he loved. M, whom they had met just hours ago, was now a significant part of them, more secured, more expressive, moreover happy. Ansh thanked his God for gifting him with a night like that, with Angie and that too with an amazing lie which successfully occupied a part of his mind throughout. Everyone was quiet as they sat in the car, Dhruv was yet to clutch the key and ignite the engine.

"How was it?" Dhruv gently asked the girls in the backseat.

"Is there any better world than wonderful?" Angie smiled, flaunting her happiness.

"Marvellous…" said Dhruv, who always claimed to have an answer to everything and was always ready to show off.

"Why are you not starting the engine, Gajju? I think we should go back now," Ansh suggested, showing him his wrist watch.

"I have a request before we go," Dhruv said, whose demands had no end. No one responded, no one opposed too, by knowing that he was the reason behind this night which they considered one of the best nights of their life. But the best was yet to come.

"I want to see the sunrise, at my secret place," Ansh was shocked as he heard this. His secret place, no one except Ansh had seen it before.

"Are you sure Gajju, you want to take the girls to that place?" Ansh said with a concern, knowing that there was no way on earth he would lead them there without any check-post.

"Yes, I need to see that now."

"What's that secret place?" Angie asked in confusion.

"Let me tell you something girls, you are going to witness the most exciting moment of your life, but try to ignore Dhruv Gajjar you meet there because he's beyond anyone's understanding," Ansh simpered. Yes, every time they go there, he was a completely different person – an immature, crazy, irresponsible gym freak would turn himself into a philosopher with some of the weirdest theories of this world.

"Let's go there." M was the first one to agree, Ansh and Angie – reading the affection in each other's eyes – were in no condition to oppose. Surprisingly, there were no policemen to stop them in the way, indicating that the omens were on their side. That secret place was near the Sabarmati river, which was rich in water after merging with Narmada. Dhruv, who was excited than ever was now swift in changing gears to reach. That was a construction site, with a guard outside. It frightened girls and as Dhruv knew this was coming, he told them that there was nothing to worry. When the guard saw Dhruv's car, he waved at him, but not after he realised they were not two, but four this time. He parked the car at his usual place and turned towards the rest.

"You guys sit here until I signal you to come out." He stepped out of the car.

He was chatting with that guard when M asked, "Is there any problem?"

"No, he is just giving him the entrance fee," Ansh answered with a smirk.

"To be precise, he is bribing him." She chortled.

"In a manner, but consider this an entrance fee."

"Do you guys come here often?"

"No, usually he likes to come alone, unless I pester him to bring me here. He can sit here for hours without talking to any one and without doing anything else."

Angie was sitting pale not knowing what was coming, just like Ansh. In a minute, Dhruv asked them to step out. They took the stairs down which took them to a heavenly place. Since it was still under construction, there were just stones everywhere and an edge, Dhruv's secret place. Yes, his secret place was nothing but a stony edge on the river. Dhruv – without asking anyone to join him – went there, folded his pant up till his knees and sat there. Ansh too joined him. It was always fascinating for them to let their feet relax in the moving water. Girls, frightened to join them, came there and stood behind.

"We don't know how to swim," both the girls said unanimously.

"Don't worry, nor do we!"Dhruv answered.

"What? Aren't you afraid?"M asked in a shock.

"Yes, and that's why it's most exciting for me! Fear is nothing but a form of anxiety and sheer excitement," Dhruv said. Within no time, the girls too folded their pants till their knees and sat beside them. What surprised them was that Angie came and sat with Ansh and M sat beside Dhruv. Angie and Ansh who were running out of words, couldn't do more than hearing a conversation that changed their lives.

"So how many bucks did you give him as bribe?" M threw a stone at Dhruv in jest.

And he replied, "A hundred per person. You call it a bribe; I call it a price for a priceless beauty which soon will fade away."

"Why?"

"They are building a riverfront here. Soon the water you are feeling down your knees will be gone,"

"Gone?"

"Yes, you will able to see the water from here, but won't be able to touch it as they will part this edge with railing. For safety purpose, but it will also take away the joy that only a few people have witnessed in their lifetime."

"What's so special about this water?"

"Can't you feel it? It's the best foot massage you'll ever get. Besides, let's start with air. Can you feel the cold breeze touching your skin and trying to ruffle your hair? It has humidity in it, which keeps it fresh and loving. People who are busy with their regular schedule, doing the same thing every day, calling it their life, hardly get to feel the joy of these things. The sun you'll see in a moment...you know it is said that if you have seen one sunrise and one sunset in a moment of peace in your entire life, you have found the purpose of your life. The moment you see darkness replacing itself with the light, it fills abundance of refreshment in your mind. Why most of the real monks choose to rise earlier than the sun? Because they can see the beauty, the power and the enlightenment it gives. Enlightenment is referred as knowledge and spiritual strength, strength which gives us the power to conquer our fears, of facing new challenges in life; and sunset, it is as important as sunrise because it teaches us that everything we possess, whether it is a person, luxuries or power in society, will somehow come to an end. There is nothing in this world you can hold forever, except yourself, so usually we do that. We hold ourselves, we try to control our desires, by ignoring our inner voice, by ignoring the natural talents we are born with, which eventually leads to frustration, irritation and anger. Soon they start hating themselves, and the moment you start hating yourself is the moment you have signed a contract with stress, sadness and sorrow to kill you. Then comes fear, and it always succeeds in conquering our excitement. Only a few are able to defeat their fear and let their excitement take charge. Have you ever stood on an edge at any high point? It will scare you, but if you notice, you'll feel your heartbeats getting faster, a part of you will always tell you to stand there forever. Just like we are sitting here right now. None of us know how to swim and we all are dealing with a great fear of falling into the river, but we all are feeling our heartbeats and we all are feeling a sense of great excitement. Now it's in your hands, you can choose to give up like most people do, or you can let your excitement take charge and enjoy the moment you have been blessed with."

"That was really deep and in a way, meaningful. But tell me the real reason why do you come here?"

"What?"

"Why do you come here? What's there inside you that you are hiding? You get philosophical to run away from the real reason that brings you here. This is the place where you, only you alone like to come and think of someone. Who's that someone? Tell me, do you miss her?"

Dhruv was in complete awe, this girl – who met him a few hours ago, knew him better than anyone, even his best friend. Yes, even Ansh was yet to find out his obsession about this place. Dhruv shrugged his shoulders and heaved a deep sigh before telling the truth.

"Yes, I do miss her."

"Tell me what do you feel?"

"About what?"

"About her, about what made you bring us here?"

"Yes, I do miss her. She is still somewhere inside of an untouched corner of my heart. She was just a school sweetheart, but we always had an unknown connection between us. She was my first female friend, so in a way she was special, but I used to see a kind of enigmatic light, something very special in her. The way she talked, the way she cared for me, the way she used to change my mood, there is no one in this world who is able to do that. Ansh is my best friend, he can catch all my lies, he can understand me better than anyone else but even he cannot do the things she was capable of. She could turn my anger into my smiles, she could understand my silence better than my words, she was able to take away all my sadness and replace it with smiles and limitless energy. Since Ansh and I came from a school where boys and girls are not allowed to be friends – and if they were, it was considered as a sin – we were usually shy. And the worst part is that there was no one around with whom guys like us could share our feelings. If we shared our feelings about anyone with our parents or siblings, they would bash us for not concentrating on our studies and for indulging ourselves into sins like these. If we shared it with our friends, they would do nothing other than bullying and make it almost impossible for you to talk to that person. It was too late when I learned that it was perfectly normal. She was gone, we were just friends and I liked her, may be secretly loved her but there was nothing I could have done. I regret it, because I could've confessed my feelings to her, without expecting anything in return. I did not know what she felt about me and it wasn't that important for me because I really was expecting nothing, but I never approached, because I was afraid of losing her as a friend. When I saw you first, I saw the same light as I used to see in her. I was shocked. Whenever I look at you, I see a glimpse of her. The only difference I see in you two is your natural blue eyes and her brownish eyes. So I decided to bring you here. Believe me, I'm not saying this for any purpose, nor is it an attempt to flirt. I'm saying what I feel and I'm feeling much more than what I'm saying."

Ansh and Angie were stunned by what Dhruv had just said.

'I didn't know he took Nirali seriously. I mean, having a secret crush is perfectly normal, but this was something beyond affection,' Ansh thought.

"I know Dhruv, you are saying the truth and there is no need to clarify your intentions. I know they are pure…at least for now." She winked and joined in the laughter with Dhruv.

"By the way, Angie, Ansh too lied about not knowing the way when you first met. Guys, I love you too, so I'm concerned about you. Don't make the mistake I made. As I said to both of you earlier, life is too short for hesitations," Dhruv said, leaving them spooky and queasy, unable to say or glance at each other.

"I think you guys need a walk together," M suggested with a smile. Without speaking a word, both of them stood up and started to walk.

They were feeling the water of Sabarmati getting louder with their anxiety. Ansh wanted to speak everything, but knowing himself through and through, he had no courage. Even though he knew she felt the same for him, words were not finding their way out. This was their moment – a moment before the sunrise. Ansh knew he had to say it before the sun comes out, but he just couldn't. He was about to ruin the moment; just then, he gathered some courage to say something.

"Angie, I know you are expecting me to say something but… sorry for lying to you on that night. I know I'll have to say that… C'mon Ansh you have to…if not now, then never…Oh gosh what am I saying…"And Ansh stopped there, realising that he had just ruined his moment, but she didn't. Angie, a person with views clear as crystal, simplest by nature, a very rare essence seen in rarest of girls, pulled out her phone and gave it to him. She had already opened a note.

On our introduction day, I was standing at the entranceway of our college. I saw a boy with luggage in his hands and his parents were following him. A lean guy, who was barely able to lift his luggage, wasn't letting his parents hold it. That impressed me. I couldn't ignore his handsome looks either. I loved you from the moment I saw you for the first time and yes, I lied and I can proudly say that I lied and I don't regret my lie. Dhruv knew this. From the very beginning, he knew it. We even talked about it quite often when you were out of our sight. Knowing that you feel the same for me, I wanted you to tell me that, by looking into my eyes, by caressing my soul and by holding my cheeks. But as days passed, I got to know of your shy nature. I realised that no matter how many signals I give, you won't propose, ever. But those things are not important as much as you are. So now here I am...saying it again – I love you Ansh! Actually, I love you too. Because, I know you do.

A drop of tear fell from Ansh's eye. Tear of shame, shame of not having the courage to do what his girl just did. He could have done it, with a little more courage, with little more guts but then he did something she needed the most. He ran his fingers into hers and held her hand, leaving his grip loose and giving her the chance to make it tighter, which is exactly what she did. Then he took her in his arms and they embraced each other, still able to hear each other's heartbeats, still making each other's clothes wet with tears, still having no intentions to leave each other, ever. That was the embrace of love, the embrace of faith, moreover the embrace of myriad affection. It was still dark; the sun was yet to rise in order to congratulate them. They returned to Dhruv and M, and sat quietly beside them, their mingled hands were enough to let them know what happened and there was no way on earth they could refrain themselves from seeing their heavenly hug.

"Congratulations buddies! I don't know if you are aware that I'm the happiest person around. Being a part of this by constantly teasing you and pestering you two was itself like an excursion," Dhruv said. Then M followed. She was a part of them now. The three musketeers were turned into fantastic four.

They saw the sun rise holding hands. They saw the darkness fading away and replacing it with light. Slowly...indicating that slow processes are more blissful and they had to let their relationship grow slowly, gradually to make it everlasting. With that sunlight, Ansh and Angie saw a dream of growing old together. That was the purpose of Ansh's life – to stand beside his girl, to make her life as special as fairytales, to grow old with her and then perish with dignity and love. They looked at the water, which was as beautiful, as romantic as it has been. Romance was in the air and completely ignorant of his best friend and newly became friend, an idea struck Ansh's mind – to kiss Angie. This was their moment.

'There would never be any better moment than this for our first kiss,' he thought.

He turned towards her and held her cheeks with his hands, just as she wanted. He was just about to touch her soft pink lips with his, when she learned his intentions and gifted a tight slap on his left cheek.

"Ouch…that was ironic Angie!" Ansh almost screamed.

"Don't even think about that Anshu! First kiss is always earned, never borrowed," she said and winked.

"You could've said it without slapping me, my love!" Ansh chuckled.

Dhruv and M guffawed on seeing this. It was already seven when they stood up to leave. There was silence on their return journey. This time, Ansh was sitting on the backseat with his girl, with her hand on his. Romantic songs kept amusing them until they fell asleep on each other's shoulder.

When they woke up, they had already reached the campus. Angie stepped out, but not before Ansh gave a gentle kiss on her head, the kiss of faith.

"Do you want to regret that you didn't ask for my number, or are you willing to live without that?" M chuckled, and smiled at Dhruv. Dhruv had always been a little egoistic when it came to asking for contact details, whether from a boy or a girl. Nevertheless, he gave her his mobile, so that she could save her number on that. She did it and stepped out, happy and charming.

I finished and looked up only to see tears dancing on Angie and Ansh's eyelids – waiting to express their way out.

"I need to go to the washroom!" Ansh said and ran out.

"I need to get some water," Angie too raced out before we could tell her that the water bottle was placed just beside her.

"Seems like I missed a chaos, M!" I said.

"Hmm, a lot happened in your absence," she said.

"Like?"

"Against her father's will, Angie said yes to marry a 'jain' guy of her Badepapa's choice."

"What? I cannot believe this…how could she?"

"She didn't have any other choice, Mithu! We cannot blame her; she cannot let her father leave his house. I'm not saying what she is doing is perfectly correct, but right now the love for her father is above everything else in this world."

I was speechless. I knew how much Angie loved her father. Although I believed that the situation would have been different if I was there. M moved my thoughts with a terrible promise, "Promise me, you'll not use my name in it. No one will ever know my name."

"What???? Then what's the point in writing the story honey! You are not making sense." Yes, that's why I've not mentioned her name. Only few close ones know about it and we are all prohibited from revealing it.

"Believe me Mithu! I'm doing it for a reason. You'll understand it someday. Now promise!"

"I'm far from even predicting that, but I promise."

M, that's what we used to call her.

That night, I had to sleep in the guest room with Ansh as my blue-eyed girl asked Angie to stay with her. I saw Ansh lying by my side; his eyes were strongly testifying that he had cried a lot in the washroom. I did not have any consoling words to offer, though I knew I had to say something. But there was one thing which was still abrupt – why was he angry with Angie? This was for her father. He should have supported her instead.

"Ansh? Why are you angry, man? I mean at first, you were the one who supported Angie in this, right?" I finally gathered the courage to ask.

"I know Gajju! I'm not angry that she is leaving me. Do you know who she is getting engaged to?"

"To whom?"

"Vishal Shah."

"What? This is insane!" I almost screamed.

"Yes, it is. Now that you understand me, good night buddy."

"Good night Ansh!" I said.

'I'll not let this happen.' I decided.

I'm still weeping, still remembering what I just read about me. These certainly are the tears of joy. Now I know, what I meant to him in the past. But, it was in the past; now we do not share the same equation. Now he already has a girlfriend, very far but he is still committed to her and I know it. There was a time when I used to turn his anger and sadness into joy with a swish. The magic is gone, not because I've lost my touch, but because the pain he's having inside is unendurable. Those who know him keep saying that he has to move on, life keeps going, but they are not the ones who have lost their loved one, he is. I've read so many stories about people losing their loved ones but none of them really gave me peace. Their narration is excellent, they direct the story well, but what I find surprising is that it was not as hard for them to move on as it is for Dhruv. I guess because they don't have to keep those bloody promises that he is trying to cope up with. He is driving me home, I'm sitting quietly, happy and at the same time, in tears.

After few a days, he is ready with the next part. We are sitting at Cafe Piano, as usual, and he starts reading.

5 February

It was the fifth day – the fifth day of February. My heartbeats were rapidly growing as I saw Valentine's Day coming near. I really did not want to have the most painful Valentine's Day of my life. It's not that we didn't give a try to start her therapies again, but she just didn't want to. She wanted to die in peace and took a word from us that no matter how bad it became, no one would call a doctor. We were left helpless – spellbound too.

I woke up and went to our room where M and Angie were still asleep. I sat beside her, took her head and kissed her lips, so passionately that Angie could not stop herself from gasping when she woke up and saw us like that. Without saying a word, she went out. I handed M an envelope.

It read,

I could not tell you if I loved you the moment I saw you
for the first time,
Perhaps it was second, third or may be the fourth, but it doesn't
matter because they all were wonderful,
Those moments are mine,
Your love is mine,
You are mine,
You cannot take that away from me.

A gentle smile followed by a passionate morning kiss was all I needed. Who cared if Angie was bothered by our kiss or not? Because they have shared countless shameless kisses in our presence, so it was our time to show them the skill they lacked – you know what I mean.

"Good morning lovebirds!" Said Angie with a generous smile as she came back. I bet there was some jealousy behind that smile.

"Morning dear!" M replied, parting our lips which I mingled in no time. Our morning kiss used to last till either of us would have a problem in breathing. That day was no exception; M gave up first and demanded her breakfast. Rightly so, she was getting more demanding with every day and I was compelled to fulfill each one of her demands. That breakfast too went without much conversation, courtesy Ansh and Angie. Even though mom and dad had done everything to restrain visitors and relatives from coming, there were few unwanted guests who kept coming. I believe they used to come so that they could know who this person was, who is calling M's parents "mom-dad" and was getting treated as their own son. Since we were busy with Ansh and Angie, it wasn't hard for mom-dad to get rid of those *guests*. That afternoon, I was smiling like a child while I was writing. Everyone sensed what was coming and everyone was swift in having his or her dinner soups. As she was having only soups at dinner, we too were having it so that she didn't have to feel different, but we knew that it wasn't working at all.

My love M, Ansh and Angie were more excited than me! They were all waiting for me to tell how our love story commenced.

And hence, I started reading.

Dhruv woke up and followed the ritual of texting M first; he texted her saying good morning. M on the other end was already awake and was staring at her phone, waiting for his message. It would not be appropriate to say that she was awake because she didn't really get a sleep. She was in love with a highly irresponsible gym freak who was exactly the opposite of her. She was a mature girl who was meant to take right decisions and she was yet to figure out what had made her fall in love with Dhruv. Apart from his perfectly sculpted physique, the only thing that could make her fall in love with him could be his straightforward nature. Dhruv too was well aware of the fact that apart from these two things, he was good for nothing, but M somehow had a strong belief that Dhruv had much more inside him than he believed he had. Dhruv considered it nothing but optimism nourished by love. They both knew they were in love with each other, but were taking their time to ensure their feelings before committing anything. Instead of being a curse like it was for Ansh and Angie, this wait was bestowing them with wonderful moments – moments that they were going to cherish for the rest of their lives. They could easily flirt with each other anytime they wanted to and they were sure of getting great replies.

After hitting the gym for two hours, Dhruv finally made a call to M through his car system.

"Hello!"

"You are one hour late."

"Was doing a cardio exercise. So you were waiting for my call that too for an hour and picked it up at the first ring?"

"May be, or maybe I was playing game on my phone."

"Nice escape, tell me what are you doing?"

"Well, I did cardio for three hours in my dreams which made me really tired so I'm thinking of getting some beauty sleep."

"You don't have lectures today?"

"I'm taking a day off, for my beauty sleep. What about you?"

"Just reached home, will make omelettes now."

"I want to taste that."

"Should I come and bring you here?"

"Aha, nope, you won't be eating only omelettes then."

"Don't worry…apart from milk and eggs, I'm a pure vegetarian. Like they say a lacto-ovo-vegetarian. Besides, I don't have any intention to eat you right now."

"I hope you remain true to your words."

"I'm a man of my words ma'am. By the way, what about a lunch together?"

"At what time?"

"I'll come to pick you up at twelve. Get ready."

Despite the fact that the conversation was had not been unusual or exceptional, M still had the feeling that this should be the day. This should be the end of her sleepless nights; this should be the demise of partial flirt and commencement of their romantic jaunt. This should be the moment of their love. They have waited for long enough – a year was enough to ensure their feelings about each other as neither of them wanted to see anyone else apart from each other. Apart from Ansh, Angie and themselves, the whole SBKS campus could swear on their lives that Dhruv and M were dating. The fantastic four was giving them enough content to gossip about, whether it was doing lunch together or running after each other on the campus roads. But they – not much concerned about what people thought and said – were having the time of their lives, which other people were missing by getting persistently envious of them.

The lunch didn't quite go as M had hoped it to. She was hoping for some flirting moments, or at best even a proposal, but nothing happened. All Dhruv talked about was either how it was getting hard for him to keep himself interested in medical subjects or it was about Ansh and Angie that how Ansh earned his first kiss and from then they were unstoppable. The only thing that amused M was when he said he sometimes gets envious of his best friend when he catches them kissing in their house. When she reached her room, she was more disappointed than tired, but not after she received a text from Dhruv which read,

I just want to see you, when you are all alone,
I just want to catch you if I can,
I just want to be there when the morning light explodes,
On your face it radiates, I can't escape,
I love you till the end…
Lines from the favourite movie of a person I love the most.

Although she wanted this at the first place and she had waited considerably long enough for this moment to arrive, she got dumbfounded for minutes when she read it. After finding herself back, she picked up her cellphone and called Dhruv.

"Dhruv, this isn't a joke, right?"

"Well, it's up to you what you make out of it."

"Don't you dare to laugh at it Dhruv!"

"I'm not; and I guess you too have waited for this."

"Ya, but I didn't expect it would come…like this!"

"What else did you think? I would be kneeling down before you, give you roses or your favourite orchids and say, I love you? C'mon baby that's too old fashioned for me."

"There is a word for that…romantic, huh!"

"But I prefer more giggling, more sizzling type of romance."

"Means?"

"Now you know the changed equation between us. I'm coming to pick you in two hours. In those two hours, you'll giggle, your nerves will fly high by thinking about what will happen when I'll hold your hand, how crazy you'll go when I'll hold you in my arms, how queasy you'll get just before the moment of our first kiss! That's how my romance works."

"I just changed, Dhruv! Need to get ready again. Call me when you reach campus."

"See, it's already working."

"Shut up Dhruv! And don't you dare to touch my lips…Bye."

And she hung up. The next two hours went exactly the way Dhruv had predicted them to be. For over fifteen minutes, she stared at the mirror until she made sure that she was looking alluring enough to hold Dhruv's eyes only to herself. She opened her wardrobe, flipped her dresses until she picked her best black one that would suit perfectly on her dove white skin. Unlike most girls around her, M wouldn't consider herself fussy in order to select what to wear, but love makes you go crazy and on that day, she couldn't imagine any other girl to be more annoying than herself. May be Angie, when she goes out on a date with Ansh but then she had enough reasons to haul the blame on love. After putting on her black dress, it was now the time to bless eye liners, blusher and her pink lipstick. She then double checked herself and made sure that her dress wasn't revealing much other than her legs below the knees, her sleeves and a slight cleavage which was going to be covered by her black jacket soon. The next one hour she spent on two things – how she would handle people around the campus when she would go out like that; and God forbid, if anyone saw her stepping in Dhruv's car and she cannot come before ten, the whole campus was going to have the gossip consignment for an entire week. Angie, her best friend, how could she escape from her sight? It was nearly impossible to get away like that; after all, she herself picked every equipment to make herself look angelic. The second thing was to stop Dhruv from kissing her. She was ready for the commitment, but a kiss? That was really a big deal for her. Not that she wasn't ready – being an adolescent, a part of her desperately wanted to feel the sensation of male lip. Knowing how lasciviously pink Dhruv's lips were, she desired them in all her dreams and they were the first reason of her sleepless nights. Being a good intellectual, she guessed right, that Angie did come across in her way and she, playing a best friend's role good enough, didn't ask a thing. But the way she sneered was enough to make M's nerves fly high. Luckily, only a few people noticed M getting out. But it was not the moment of fear for her; what frightened her was the sound of her heart beats when she stepped into the car. She was trying hard to control her gasps, hoping that Dhruv wouldn't notice it.

Instead of taking her into a lavish restaurant as usual, Dhruv broke his ritual by taking her into his house. M who was now making clear sounds with every breath she took, couldn't do anything other than sitting pale. As she walked out of the car and followed Dhruv inside, he led her to the dining room. She exhaled audibly. May be she was frightened by the thought of following Dhruv to his bedroom. When she entered the dining room, she saw her favourite purple orchids placed on the table with a steel plate cover at its centre. He then took the cover off to let her see the perfectly shaped, sliced into pieces omelette which had kept its warmth due to the hot-plate facility on the table. After offering her a seat, Dhruv settled down at the opposite side and served her a piece to eat. She cut the slice with the butter-knife, fork and blessed her ravenous mouth.

"This is the only thing I'm so good at, so couldn't take any chances. Hope you like it," Dhruv spoke the first words with a generous smile. M, without looking at him, nodded and fed herself another piece. Dhruv stood up, reached where M was sitting and placed his hand on hers without moving it from its place.

"Let's get to the point M! I'm a terrible student who barely manages to pass, a gym freak who spends his productive hours in gym to pump his muscles, an irresponsible guy with whom no girl would want to spend an entire life, and a completely spoiled brat. And this spoiled brat is in love…in love with a girl who is an extraordinary student for starters, a girl who is mature and nearly perfect in taking her decisions, who understands life and its value really well. Basically, a perfect girl whom everyone desires to be with…and this irresponsible spoiled nerd is madly in love with you. Can you come to his life and give him a purpose – a purpose to live and not just breathe." Dhruv proposed by looking straight into her eyes, giving her a shot of trust, commitment. At first, M couldn't believe that the moment of truth had arrived; he had finally said it. Not by kneeling down, not by doing any cheesy stuff or funny business, but by looking straight into her eyes, indicating that this was the romance he preferred – by just holding her hand, giving her a shot of faith indicating that he was now ensured and ready for the commitment; that this was not the infatuation driven by lust. This was the desired dream of growing old together. She tilted her head to one side, as a hint of smile was playing on her lips. Her accelerated heartbeats slowed down and she finally uttered some words.

"Do I have any other choice? I too am madly in love with that crazy, stupid, idiotic nerd, and I will till my last breath." Just as Dhruv was waiting for the opportunity, he took her in his arms and hugged her. Before she could come out from the sensation of that heavenly hug, Dhruv planted his lips on hers. M, by the time had completely forgotten that she was supposed to stop him. The only thing on her mind was that this was the end of her sleepless nights. She had the first kiss of her life and that too with the person who loved her completely. She had no doubt about her feelings for him because for over a year they had tested their feelings for each other. She was completely carried away in the wind of his love that came as a twister and was now showering its love on her lips, leaving her entire body shivering. After that everlasting smooch, they knew they had to stop themselves, they knew they were not ready to make love from their souls even though their bodies, wandering and floating in lust were demanding it. They parted their lips with heavy hearts and embraced each other again. Later that night, when M invented the suffix 'Mithu' for Dhruv, she knew that he would like this name as much as she liked it for him. Ansh and Angie, who were suspecting this, decided to catch them red handed. So, after Dhruv went to a sleep, Ansh stole his phone and read all his romantic conversation with M, which Dhruv being a lazy lad had forgotten to delete. The next day, before the newly committed couple could confess anything in front of them, Ansh and Angie had enough stock to laugh at them and as always, to make other spectators envious of the fantastic four.

For the first time that day, I saw Ansh and Angie smiling together. No matter how hard they tried, they couldn't hide the affection and care towards each other. I could see their love underneath Angie's disappointments and Ansh's anger. They were trying to restrain themselves from looking into each other's eyes, but were consistently failing.

"Ansh, Angie, can you please wait outside for some time? It's our promise time," M mumbled. Without saying a word, they left the room.

"So now, what's the order for me, ma'am?" I sneered.

"Promise me! You won't die single. You'll fall in love again and will give your full commitment to her like you did to me."

"I'm already in love baby! Is it possible to love two people at the same time?" I said sternly.

"I know you would not fall for anyone, but you'll have to. This is the end of my life, not yours. Please understand Mithu!" A pleading sense was there in her voice.

For over five minutes, I said nothing. She too didn't bother me. She knew I was taking my time to think and this wasn't easy back then. It isn't easy even now.

"Only at one condition,"

"What condition?"

"You promise me that you'll send someone for me."

"I promise Mithu!"

"Don't make the promises you can't keep, baby! You are not going to keep it," I said without slurring a word. She too noticed it and frowned.

"But you'll have to. I will be there to look after you. I'll be somewhere in the flashlight, I will be there in the sunlight you'll feel in the morning. I'll be inside those breezes which will make you feel alive. I'll be inside your heart to make you feel happy about little things. In your successes and failures, in your ups and downs, I'll be there to provide you strength. I will be there to watch you keeping your promises. Get it, Mithu?"

"Yes, ma'am." I coyly nodded.

When I was trying to sleep beside Ansh in the guest room, the only thing running in my mind was, *I don't think I'll be able to keep this promise.*

"I don't think I'll be able to keep that promise," I hold his hand as he says.

"You will, trust me." That's all I could say.

"It's easier said than done, Nilu!" Harshness in his voice makes me frown. But I don't react; I know he doesn't mean it.

But he goes on…

"Sorry Nilu, but you should not comment on something you haven't experienced." That was it. I couldn't take more

"Dhruv, you think I'm here for any personal gain?"I look straight at him, to remind him that this is not something I deserve.

"I didn't say that, Nilu!"

"Didn't deny it either, Dhruv! Let me tell you one thing clearly. Yes, I can't see you like this and I want you to move on in life, but I would never ever coerce you to feel anything for me against your will, and I mean it. We are best friends, we grew up together, so the first thing I want for you is to be happy, even if your happiness lies in someone else's arms." This is the last thing I would desire, but yes, what I said was true.

"Sorry Nilu! I know I've been a jerk. You have been my true friend and no matter what life brings to us, you shall be like that, always." I don't find his words consoling. May be I am tired of being just a friend. May be…

"I need to go now Dhruv! Can you mail me the next part?" I say and stand up.

"Okay, and Nilu! Sorry again! I wish I could ever repay what you've done for me so far." He says with his head down. He is guilty; I can see it in his eyes.

"I'm not doing it to get anything in return, Dhruv! I'm doing it…" I didn't finish the sentence,

"Because I love you."I mumble without checking if he heard me or not – wishing that he did. Back in my house, I open the mail Dhruv has sent me.

6 February

"Because I love you." My morning commenced with those beautiful words. No, they were not from M; my best friend was uttering the words for the girl he loved. I knew if I'd open my eyes, they would stop talking and probably it was the first time they were actually talking to each other. I was in no mood to be a party spoiler, so I kept my eyes closed and let my ears do the job.

"The only reason I'm mad at you is because I love you. I should hate you for what you are doing. I should tear you apart from my life, but a part of me still loves you and you are not the one I'm angry at… it's myself that I want to kill. I should be stronger, but the part of me that loves you is making me feel weaker and helpless." There was a minute of silence after Ansh said that, maybe they were checking if I was awake or not. I just didn't move an inch, nor did I open my eyes.

"Ansh, you were the one who supported me in this at first. Was it a lie when you said you would sacrifice anything – even me for my father?"There was a cry in her voice that struck me hard in my chest.

"Yes, I said that and I meant it when I said it. I'm not angry because you are going away from me. I'm angry at the thought that you are ready to marry a guy who almost killed your father? You know if anyone else would be there, I'd happily let you go without regret, but sorry, I cannot be a part of this crime you are committing. You are cheating your father and me. I cannot smile watching you do that," Ansh snorted, as if he was squeaking hard with his remaining voice after screaming the whole night.

"I wasn't a cheater, Ansh! I just wanted to be a good daughter and a good lover, but I failed as both," Angie's sad voice faded away with those lines.

I stood up. Ansh wasn't surprised at seeing me awake, as if he already knew.

"You heard that right?"

"Not much, and don't worry, I won't be bothering you. Tell me, where are my orchids?" He gave me the orchids, fresh, odourless and beautiful – just as she liked. I prepared the envelope and settled everything on the white tray. When Angie met me on the way, smirked by seeing this incarnation of mine – and I simpered at hers.

I again ran my fingers on her forehead and kissed it. M was just waiting for my touch and slowly opened her blue eyes and…miracle! That was the only suffix that could suit her eyes. I was playing with the envelope, knowing what was inside which her sixth sense had already noticed. She tried hard to snatch it from my hand, but there was no way in heaven I'd give her that before the morning kiss. Just after licking away every bit of sleep from her mouth, I handed her the envelope.

It read,

Your pink panoptic lips, throwing an everlasting smile all the time,
If only I knew I'd lose them,
I'd never stop myself from kissing you,
I'd never stop my tongue from exploring every available taste

> *and then finally meet your tongue,*
> *If only I knew that…*
> *You still cannot take that away from me.*

She gave me a quick signal that she wanted to be kissed, she wanted me to put all my words into reality and I followed her signal with obeisance. Only then did I get the energy to make the perfect omelettes for everyone.

Ansh and Angie both went home in the afternoon, promising to come again the next day. They couldn't hear the part I was writing – at least not now, in each other's presence. We had a howling family time in the afternoon. For the past few days, lunch and dinner sessions had been quiet in the presence of Ansh and Angie. In a terse manner, they had been spoiling our family time. M was ready to hear me at seven. Usually the narration begins at nine, but that day was special. We both were alone there, without any interruption, without any ignominious glance and without any broken stripes.

And I started reading.

Ansh's head started spinning when he woke up and found himself alone and that too on his birthday. He was already agitated by not having a call from his love, Angie. He knew the conversation went cheeky but he deserved it after a year of being in a relationship. And for god's sake, it wasn't for the first time! He tried to recall the conversation of last night before the clock struck twelve.

"Tell me Ansh! What do you want on this birthday?"

"You know very well Angie! I want you."

"Shut up, Ansh!"

"It's been a year now, Angie! I can't be so unromantic like you."

"You are not being romantic Ansh, you are being desperate."

"What? How can you say that? Well, maybe a little, but I think I deserve it."

"Okay, I'll think about it."

"Please, my love."

"I told you I'll think about it Ansh. Don't push me. And who's in a hurry?"

"I am. And someone else is too,"

"And who is that?"

"Come here, I'll show you. I can't wait to introduce you two."

"No, keep it with you. It suits you better. I have work to do Ansh, bye."

And she hung up. Didn't call him; didn't even text him. That was awkward. They've had more cheeky flirtations than that and each time she fully enjoyed it.

'Then why is she ruining the big day?'

He called Dhruv but got no response from him as well. After having cake bath last night, he must have gone to drop their friends to the hostel.

"Friends are friends, you can't spoil all my day Angie!" Groaned Ansh and stepped down to eat the remaining cake and to make some omelettes. He didn't know he would be astounded enough to lose his breath once he stepped down and saw Angie sitting on the dining table with a new cake, candles and rose petals around it, covering the cake with its heart shape. Dumbstruck Ansh couldn't do anything other than to just stare at Angie, who was waiting for him since eternity. Ansh was cursing himself for thinking unfavourable things about Angie in his mind. It was his birthday; there had to be a surprise. Without saying a word, he sat beside her quietly.

"Happy birthday, my love…" She said with twinkling eyes.

"So, this was your plan. Where are Gajju and M?"

"To get some coffee, and to bring lunch for us," she coyly replied.

"Oh Angie! You choreographed everything for me? How sweet!" Ansh giggled.

"It was a team effort. Dhruv and M came up with the idea."

"Friends are friends," mumbled Ansh.

"So, to whom were you getting desperate to introduce me?"She arched a brow at him, moving her eyes provocatively, which aroused Ansh in no time.

"Before that, I'm going to eat my cake. And by that I mean you," Ansh said and ran his fingers into hers. Angie exhaled loudly in nervousness.

"Can I lift you Angie?"Ansh meekly asked.

"Can you?"Angie simpered. Within no time, she was in his arms. As a lean guy, he struggled at first, but – as he was charged with gallons of testosterone – managed at last.

"So this is my gift?"

"Hmm… Your pie is ready, have it." She said with a wink and kissed his cheeks.

Then they hugged each other, tightly – as if they would never leave each other. They were feeling the abundance of love in each other's arms. They didn't require words to say 'I love you', and they didn't require wings to fly. The moment itself was heavenly, but not after Ansh's phone rang. It was Dhruv, Ansh showed it to Angie. "Put it on speaker," she demanded.

"What?" Ansh snorted.

"Reached our bedroom?" He chuckled and the in-love couple looked at each other in disguise.

"How do you know?"

"Haha… Just guessing man, calculating time and guessing your actions. What do you suspect? A spy cam? By the way I have a gift for you. Open our wardrobe and check your drawer."

Both went up to check his drawer and found a pack of condoms.

"What is this?" Ansh came up with the most stupid question.

"This is exactly what you need right now, and if you excuse me from your idiotic questions, I also have a date going on here," Dhruv said and hung up the call.

Angie threw a shy smile at Ansh. No matter how much they were angry on Dhruv for spoiling the moment, they both knew that he had done them a favour.

"Shall we?" Ansh asked for her hand. He lifted her again and led her to bed. They started kissing when Angie's phone rang. M!! She showed him and picked up.

"Hello?"

"Hi madam."

"Have you guys finished kissing?" M asked with a naughty smile.

"What's all this M? Are you guys taking revenge?"

"Haha, sort of. By the way I've got a surprise for you too. Open your purse."

Angie opened her purse, and pulled out everything one by one. The only thing she found new there was a silk scarf.

"What's this?" Ansh asked.

"She knows exactly what it is, Ansh," M said and hung up the phone.

"What is this for?" Ansh asked, being clueless.

"When we had a discussion about sex in the hostel, we discussed about it, and that bitch told me then she would gift me one."

"What discussion?"

"When you are having sex for the first time, every girl is scared; in this condition a blindfold can be useful and well, it is more sensuous this way. It can lessen your pain, shyness and give you the chance to feel every touch of your partner." She looked down as she finished.

"So you want us to try this?" This was tempting for Ansh.

"I don't mind," she shyly murmured.

Then he folded that scarf on her eyes and lifted her again. "I wish I don't have to lift you again today, my arms are already hurting."

He softly whispered, she laughed; knowing that Ansh was going to undress her soon. The very thought was shaking her body in shyness.

"Is this your first time?" Ansh quipped, expected a slap in return, but got a frowned face instead.

"I'm sorry about that Ansh!" She softly spoke, Ansh widened his eye. Completely shaken, not by the fact that she wasn't a virgin, but it came in a situation like this.

"It's okay Angie, tell me, who was he?" He was somehow able to hold myself.

"Not one, there were two."

What?????????

"Do you want to talk about it?" Whatever her past was, at the moment, comforting her was the first thing on Ansh's mind.

"Are you going to leave me after that?" Angie asked.

"No Angie, no! Actually yes, I'm sad, but only because you didn't tell me before. When I first saw you and fell in love with you, I desired only you, not the virgin you." She embraced him in her arms as an affirmation to make love.

Now there was no secret left and they loved each other more than ever. Yes, she wasn't a virgin and yes, it made their faith towards each other stronger.

"This is my first time, so you are going to teach me the best ways," Ansh whispered in her ear. She then asked him to run his fingers on her back. Ansh – for the first time touching a female body – blessed his fingers by touching her bare-silken back and she followed the same. Then only she ascertained about the sensitivity of his back. Ansh felt an instant tickle as she touched his bare back. She too realised it and teased him by rolling her nails and fingers more, when he couldn't take it anymore.

"Stop it Angie!"

"Tell me if you don't like it Ansh, and I'll stop."

Did not like it? He loved each erogenous action!

"I love it, but I think you will get your whole life to do that."

And they bumped their heads in laughter.

"Kiss me on my neck," she demanded, and he followed, sensing certain tenderness in her movement.

"Kiss me on my head," she demanded, and he followed.

"Kiss me on my cheeks."

"Kiss me on my lips."

After that everlasting kiss, she asked him to undress her. She was wearing a black top and blue jeans. Ansh was running his fingers slowly and precisely, so that she could feel every bit of his touch. He gently removed everything as she had asked and there she was, the woman he loved, naked – with only a silk scarf on her eyes. Then they made love. How could Ansh forget that his girlfriend was an amazing liar? Yes, she lied; she did bleed when he penetrated her. She cried in pain when Ansh went inside her for the first time and as Ansh – a man who did not believe in only seeking pleasure but also giving it – had done all the research about that G-spot and female orgasm so with his hand, tongue and with the hand of his research, Ansh made her reach her orgasm three times. She was completely exhausted and shaken in pleasure with that third orgasm.

They lay naked on the bed and were still determined not to leave each other.

"You bloody liar! Why did you lie?" Ansh asked after unfolding her scarf.

"Consider this a test in which you passed with flying colours." She smiled and kissed him on his chest.

"What if I had failed?"

"Then I would have left you right here." She didn't smile this time.

"Really? I mean in between?" Ansh chuckled.

"Yes, you have any doubt?" No, he didn't. Angie, a person with her views clear as crystal on everything, was the love of his life and he was proud to have a girl like her.

"But I passed, right?" Ansh simpered.

"Yup, with flying colours." She giggled.

"So what do I get as a reward?"

"Is there anything more I can give you?"

"Yes, my angel-eyes."

"They are all yours." She winked, and they did it again. This time, more passionately with his angel-eyes.

Dhruv and M came back with Domino's pizza and coke. Boys were setting up everything on the table and they could hear the girls giggling and laughing upstairs – obviously the gossip topic being their love-making.

"Was it that great?" Dhruv smirked.

"Don't ask," Ansh replied with a wink.

"Now you owe me a favour," he blurted.

"What favour?" Ansh asked tersely.

"Don't split a word about what I'm going to do next," he admonished.

'What for?' Ansh could smell something really bad.

"What is in your mind Gajju?" Ansh was frightened with Dhruv's devilish smile.

"Watch out," he said – went inside and came up with a bottle of vanilla flavoured vodka.

"What the hell man, are you nuts?" Ansh snarled. Dhruv signalled him to remain calm. "Are you trying to intoxicate our girls?" He wasn't calm at all. How could he be?

"Yes, that's the only way for me to get laid. I want you to return me a favour, keep quiet, unless you want your best friend to graduate as a virgin," he said. This was not right. Was it? He didn't know. But

Ansh chose to support his friend. Dhruv then emptied about thirty percent of coke and replaced it by filling vodka inside. For a one-and-a-half litre coke bottle, this wasn't just adequate, it was high… especially for the girls who had never tasted it.

The girls came down and got settled on their chairs. They didn't realise that the taste was any different at first and Dhruv smartly cut down all the chances of them to notice by dropping ice cubes in their glasses. Ansh did his job, he kept quiet. They seemed to like it. Both the girls consumed three straight pegs and asked for more.

"Do you know something Angie?" tipsy M uttered.

"What M?"

"Our boyfriends got us sloshed."

'What? She knew? How?' Ansh arched his eyes at Dhruv but he looked as ambivalent as Ansh was.

"And you know why Angie? Because he wants to fuck me! Right baby?" She glanced at Dhruv with anger. He looked down in shame. She slowly stood up and sat in Gajju's lap and kissed him on his cheeks.

"If you wanted this so badly, why didn't you just ask? Why did you do all this stuff?"

"Sorry M! My intentions were not to…" Gajju started giving his rational explanations, but with all their astonishment, Angie filled another glass.

"Whatever it is, I'm liking it," she said and consumed it in seconds.

"Yes, I want another too," M said and followed.

After emptying all of that vodka mixed coke, their eyes went groggy. The guys were just observing their moves. After all, they had seen drunken girls for the first time in their life.

"Hey M! Look at Ansh's shirt. Cool no?" Angie uttered.

"Yes, why should boys have all the fun? We should wear that too. Dhruv! Tell us where your wardrobe is?" she demanded.

"M, come and sit down…"

"Your wardrobe, Dhruv!" She demanded, exceeding her aggression.

"Upstairs!" Dhruv answered in helplessness.

They both went upstairs. Ansh looked at Dhruv with impeccable amount of anger.

"Sorry bro!"

"Does it matter now?" He couldn't even say, 'I told you so!' because he didn't. They waited about five minutes and heard them stepping down.

Guys' eyes widened like saucers after what they saw. They saw girls wearing their full sleeve shirts with folded sleeves and well, just shirts. Yes, everything below their six inches of thighs, which their shirts were covering, was visible. They were staggering while walking which were making their shiny white legs even more salient. This was fascinating. Ansh and Dhruv both were trying hard not to look at each other's girls but some things are beyond human control and this was one of those.

Angie came over, sat on Ansh's lap and whispered, "I love you Anshu!" She kissed him on his neck, which made him feel diffident, and he glanced at Dhruv. He was holding M in his arms. She was already asleep.

"Let's do it again Anshu!" Angie whispered again and kissed his lips. Ansh too got carried away – forgetting about the presence of his best friend – and kissed her deeply. After they finished, Ansh looked up. Dhruv was standing there – waiting for him to finish.

"You go upstairs. I'm staying here." He said and took M to the living room and gently placed her on the sofa.

Ansh tried to copy him and lifted Angie in his arms.

"Third time, thanks to you bastard!" He grinned. Dhruv smiled back and they went upstairs.

After a five-hour sleep, Ansh woke up. Angie was already awake, had already freshened up and changed her clothes. Hopefully, she well remembered what happened and she was not miffed at Ansh. He felt relieved. They stepped down and went to the living room and saw Dhruv sleeping there on the sofa with M in his arms.

"Aww, how romantic!" Angie mumbled with her cute voice.

"And erotic too!" Ansh winked referring to M's revealing legs. Angie slapped him on his arm and held his hand.

Who would have thought that Ansh would be the one getting benefit from Dhruv's plan instead of him?

'Yeah! That's what luck is all about,' Ansh mumbled.

I looked up and saw M throwing her naughty smile at me.

"Ansh and Angie are going to kill you," she guffawed.

"Don't worry ma'am, I have their written consent," I meekly answered.

"Mithu! I've penned some lyrics for you. Can you please cite them for me?"

"Of course ma'am," I bowed my head in obedience and stood up.

"It's in the drawer." She pointed her finger at the wardrobe. I opened it, pulled the drawer out and took a paper from it. I smiled as I saw the lyrics. I stood beside her and started singing with the worst singing skills of mine.

If I ever leave this world alive
I'll thank you for all the things you did in my life
If I ever leave this world alive
I'll come back down and sit beside your
feet tonight
Wherever I am you'll always be
More than just a memory
If I ever leave this world alive

If I ever leave this world alive
I'll take on all the sadness
That I left behind
If I ever leave this world alive
The madness that you feel will soon subside
So in a word don't shed a tear
I'll be here when it all gets weird
If I ever leave this world alive
So when in doubt just call my name
Just before you go insane
If I ever leave this world
Hey I may never leave this world
But if I ever leave this world alive
He says I'm okay, I'm alright,
Though you have gone from my life
You said that it would,
Now everything should be all right
He says I'm okay; I'm alright,
Though you have gone from my life
You said that it would,
Now everything should be all right
Yeah should be all right.

"You changed the lyrics M!"

"Just a couple of letters, Mithu! But so relevant to our situation, no?" She simpered.

I remained silent; in tears.

"Seems like I'll have to put my cancer cells inside your tears, so they start hiding instead of shedding." She smiled again and I missed a beat, again.

"You know I would gladly embrace them. Anything more for you ma'am?" I bowed at her.

"Yes, the promise!"

I nodded and she continued, "Promise me! You'll regain your fitness and become that old handsome Dhruv Gajjar again."

"Haha… With pleasure ma'am, I promise."

"By the way, do you remember from where I got these lyrics?"

"How can I forget that wonderful day, M?" I winked.

After two hours, she opened her eyes. She was wearing my shirt, only the shirt. My eyes were locked and confused in between her soft pink lips, her sharp blue eyes, her smooth silky hair and last but not the least, her milky white legs. Two hours passed in those coupled minutes, as I was lost in observing my girl's beauty while holding her hand. These things are more fascinating than sex.

"Was I asleep?" She asked with groggy eyes, adding another fragrance to her beauty.

"Yes, my love."

"My head is paining atrociously Mithu!"

"I know baby. It's a trademark of hangover. Let me take care of it," I pulled her head down to my lap and started massaging it gently while kissing in between.

"Where are Ansh and Angie?"

"They are upstairs. Making out – third time."

"Do you want to Mithu?"

"Yes, but not now! Only when my queen will demand it."

"I'm demanding baby! Let's do it."

"You don't need to lie, my love. I can clearly see that you are not ready. I felt sorry about getting you drunk…but now I don't. This is enough for me." I winked and put my fingers on her legs and let them run. She giggled and moved closer to embrace me in her arms and gently whispered in my ear. "I love you Mithu!"

And I replied back, with a passionate kiss. After that she started playing, with my buttons.

"*What am I supposed to do now? In your shirt?*" She was trying everything to test my patience.

"*This is immensely tempting baby! But what about a movie?*"

And she punched me on my chest. I switched on the TV and started to switch channels. She suddenly held my hand.

"*Wait Mithu! That's my favourite movie!* P.S. I Love You…"

It had just started. Gerry was dancing semi-nude trying to please his Holly. I winked at M. We had discussed this scene so many times and I promised her to perform a strip dance for her. Then M almost jumped on my lap when Holly got the first letter from Jerry.

"*Don't worry M! You will receive these same letters after my death,*" I chuckled. She patted my back.

"*I'm going to die first.*"

"*Forget it M! I am.*"

"*No, I am.*"

We fought for a while on that. Then the beauty of Ireland just took our breath away; at the park where Gerry and Holly first met. M held my hand, even tighter at the moment.

"*Mithu! If possible, we'll go to Ireland for our honeymoon.*"

"*Of course we will, my love!*"

"*And will take a walk in the same park.*"

"*Just walk? I was thinking about making out right there.*" I chuckled, she guffawed.

"*Your kind suggestion will be considered.*" She winked, and I kissed her.

A beautiful end left tears in M's eyes. Filmy! But it did me a favour. She gifted me an everlasting passionate kiss. We were lost in each other's lips, tongues and arms but suddenly some beautiful lyrics amused us.

If I ever leave this world alive…

What if there is a secret residing within you that you are not allowed to share with anyone? What if there is someone who you are missing badly and yet you have to believe that they are complete strangers to you? It hurts – even to me it does.

We are sitting at Angie and Ansh's place to hear the further narration. After having scrumptious food cooked by Dhruv and Ansh, we sit in their room.

He pulls out his Mac and starts reading.

7 February

In front of M that day, was a plate not full of her favourite orchids, but of lush red roses. She opened the envelope and there was nothing in this world capable of stopping her from breaking into tears.

You can touch these roses now, ravishingly beautiful just as you,
You can smell the perfume it produces, just the way you do,
Soon, they will wither and die, just the way you will
You can take that away from me.

"Mithu!"
"Hmm?"

"Tell me how much you cried while writing this?"

I didn't answer. My answer was dumped in the dustbin around the corner. I pointed my hand to the dustbin where she saw over fifty torn pages and grinned from ear to ear. What she forgot to notice was they were all wet.

"I'm going to kill you, Dhruv!" Angie growled and ran after me from the bed. She finally read her lovemaking part and was confusingly miffed at me. Yes, confusingly, with a pleasured smile on her face. She wondered how I got so much information about them. The answer was obvious. The person, who was still in love with her, truly madly and deeply, provided it. She too knew it and wanted to hear it. M and I were enjoying her visible blush when I told her that she provided every romantic, erotic, dirty detail to her ex-boyfriend who was soon going to marry her. Yes, I would drag them both to their wedding.

Ansh didn't come over that day. He knew he could narrate everything to me over the phone or in person, but he could not bear me express his feelings when Angie was around. Angie somehow had the courage for that – and I wonder for how long that would last. After having the delicious sweet-corn soup – obviously cooked by me, they both were prepared to hear the narration, about which M and I had been constantly teasing Angie.

I started reading

"What dude? Are you nuts?" Half of the food was spitted out from Dhruv's mouth as Ansh told him his ridiculous decision. He was going to do 'Aththai Tap'- a fast where one cannot eat for eight straight days and is only allowed to drink only boiled water, and that too before sunset. Angie was doing it, and after trying everything to restrain her – he failed. Her family had already made the announcement and she too was keen on doing it, so did Ansh. Dhruv felt like he almost dropped his ears and could not believe his friend's foolishness and he too, as a wise friend was trying to stop him.

"Dude, are you nuts?" He continued… "Eight days without food and just on boiled water? This is suicide, man!"

"I know Gajju and that's why I'm not going to let her do that alone," Ansh firmly answered.

"Ansh, what she is going to do will be considered as a *tapasya*. Your attempt will be considered as only starvation. We'll be in Ahmedabad on weekends, so you think that your mom will let you do that?" Dhruv's question was obvious and logical, which made Ansh think for a while.

"I'm going to stay here this time," he declared. Dhruv again tried to convince him and the argument lasted for several minutes, but just as Ansh had failed to convince Angie, Dhruv failed with Ansh.

"Then I'm going to stay with you too," Dhruv said.

"No bro, you don't need to. I'll manage by myself here." He surely didn't want to trouble Dhruv in this task.

"Done talking? Now listen! I'll be here with you for these eight days of your so called "fast". You will be resting all day long. You won't even stand up to drink water, understood? Otherwise, I'm not going to let you do it." Gajju sternly announced; Ansh couldn't help but nod.

The first day went easy for them. Ansh and Angie set some rules to survive eight days without food. Like they would not talk over the phone as it would make them more hungry and thirsty. They decided to use the technology of Skype with which they could see each other anytime they would want. Being a Jain, Angie had the experience of fasting where being a Brahmin, fasting for Ansh had always been eating fruits, salads and wafers. By evening, Ansh started having headache and dizziness, but he didn't tell anyone about it. Not even his best friend Dhruv. On the second day, he could not hide it. His head started spinning and he could barely wake up. Everyone around him – Dhruv, Angie, M started worrying and tried to make him end the fast, but he was keen to do it. He wanted to feel the same hunger and pain that his girl was feeling. The only thing that was helping him to go through it was that he could see Angie on the screen and could feel her around. The third day got worse. He could not even move. Angie even disconnected Skype after having a belligerent war of words with him. She started cursing herself for allowing Ansh to do it. She was sitting on her bed, weeping on the foolishness of his boyfriend, when her father – Mr. Prasoon Shah, an open minded and an extremely friendly dad, unlike a common Indian father – saw her. At first, he thought it was because of hunger, but when she told him that her boyfriend was doing a fast for her, at first he couldn't believe his ears. But when he saw Ansh, almost dying, he was proud of her daughter's choice. Not because of the hunger strike that the stupid boy was doing, but when he talked to him, he saw a genuine, caring guy who could look after his daughter...perhaps better than him. It was he who convinced Ansh to end his fast by saying that he was planning to introduce him to his brother and father, so he needed him to be fit and attentive. Ansh unwillingly decided to end his fast, but that too on the next day. The others didn't have any choice but to agree. On the eve of the fourth day, Ansh ended his fast with lemon juice. Dhruv and M did his *parna*, which Angie watched live on the screen. Later that night, the lovebirds were chirping romantically, thanking their destiny for giving Angie a best friend in the form of her father Mr. Shah. They were convinced they would not have to face any hurdles in their marriage now. The only person Angie feared was her Badepapa, who was exactly opposite to Mr. Shah – extremely unfriendly and a highly conservative person. He and his son Rishi were the only living hurdles for them. Eight days of Athai Tap finally came to an end and the lovebirds could not wait to see each other at Angie's parna function.

"I think this should be the place. You two go inside if you wish, while I park the car," Dhruv said as they reached the given address.

"No, we are waiting here, we'll go inside together," M said. Dhruv, returned a smile and headed for the parking.

As the three of them entered, they saw Mr. Shah standing outside the door to greet them. He embraced them and escorted them inside. Ansh saw Angie's grandfather, Badepapa and her first cousin Rishi standing there. Ansh had seen their picture before, so he could easily identify them. Clearly, Mr. Shah was giving Ansh the extra caring treatment, which bothered them. A kind of disdain started developing in their eyes for Ansh. Then Ansh saw his girl, sitting in a traditional dress, looking gorgeous as always. She blushed at seeing Ansh and he felt another pinch of sugar. She was sitting on a stage. Everyone was coming to her, pouring different kinds of liquids and doing her 'parna'.

"I think she is expecting you three on stage," Mr. Shah generously said, teasing Ansh for stalking his daughter. Ansh nodded and the three of them went up. As she saw Ansh coming, Angie started moving her eyes and lips provocatively and then bit her lip, a sheer turn on for Ansh.

"Stop provoking me like this, my love!" Ansh muttered in her ears.

M poured the liquids and they returned back to their seats.

After five minutes, a voice came from behind them, "Excuse me!" Ansh turned back and saw Rishi standing there.

"Yes?" He politely asked.

"My father wants to see you all. Follow me." As they went inside the room, they saw Angie's father, grandfather and Badepapa standing there.

"Bapuji, he is Anshul, the boy I was telling you about," Mr. Shah said, pointing his finger towards Ansh.

"What is your full name, boy?" Badepapa asked, not so gently.

"Anshul Bhatt, sir!" He softly answered.

"A Brahmin? Prasoon, you chose a Brahmin boy for Angel?" Angie's Badepapa growled at Mr. Shah. The three of them were standing quiet, pale.

"What's wrong with that *motabhai* (big brother)? He is a well-educated, well-cultured and well-natured boy," Ansh held his head high after hearing those praises.

"He is not Jain, *kaka* (uncle). How could you forget that outcast marriages are forbidden in our Jain community?" Rishi growled at his uncle.

'This is not something that Jainism enjoins.' Ansh scoffed in his mind.

Angie's grandpa was standing quietly, just like Ansh, Dhruv and M.

"Look son! She is my daughter and I know what is right for her and my decision is final," Angie's father replied firmly.

"Since when did you start taking decisions, Prasoon? And you three, get out! This is our family matter, none of your business." Badepapa admonished and the three of them walked out.

Later that evening, thoughts were waving like nightmares in Ansh's mind.

'I'm waiting for Angie's message or call since morning. I know this is going to be really hard for her, but one thing is clear, no matter what, I'm going to support her. I'm going to stand by her side in her every decision. Even if she decides to break up with me, I won't question her even once. That I promise to myself.'

Just then, Ansh's phone beeped.

"We need to talk, call me as soon as possible." Read Angie's message.

Without any second thoughts, Ansh hit the call button.

"How's everything baby?"

"Not good Ansh. In fact, worse than we could have imagined!"

"How?"

"After you left, papa had a big quarrel with Badepapa and Rishi bhai,"

"And?"

"Badepapa said if he wants to support us and our relationship, then he must cut all strings with our family and leave the house. We will also be ostracized from our community."

"What? How? I mean, how can he do that? To his own young blood? And what did your grandpa say??"

"He stood silent, as always."

"We also noticed his silence. Now what, Angie?"

"Papa is ready to leave the house, but I can't let him Ansh! He gave twenty years of his life to our family business. Still, he doesn't have a single property to his name. He has no financial backup, he never asked for anything from Badepapa, and so he never got anything. He used to say that Mom was his biggest investment and I his best return. Now I have got to choose, Ansh! Forsake him or you. One of us will have to sacrifice, either you and me or papa,"

"We can't let him suffer, Angie. I was waiting for your message or call all day, but one thing was firm in my mind, one thing I promised myself that no matter what, and I mean it, no matter what! I'll stand by you and your decision."

"Thanks Ansh!"

"Hey baby, please don't cry! See we had our moments, right? You know I'll feel privileged to do it for papa. Whatever time we spent together, it was like a dream for me. But if you think this as our only option, I'm with you, no matter what."

"Need to go Ansh, bye."

"Bye."

'The love between our conversations is already dropped. It was easy to say those philosophical lines, but I know this is going to be hard. Maybe even impossible to live with. But I can't blame her; she is right at her place. I have to make up my mind for the fact that you can't keep what's not yours, you can't hold on to something that doesn't want to stay. I just can't – and again, no matter what, I'm going to keep my word.'

These things were on Ansh's mind when his phone started ringing; it was Gajju.

"Bro, Angie's father wants to meet us tomorrow. I've called him at Cafe Piano. I'll come to pick you."

"Okay." Ansh answered and hung up.

'What could it be now? I shouldn't give up. Maybe there is still some hope left. Maybe, this is not the end of my story. Maybe, this is not an end. Maybe, this is just an eternal middle. Let's wait for the next day.'

Ansh mumbled and went to bed, in tears.

As I looked up, I saw Angie in tears, looking down. M and I reached for her hand, took her in our arms and she started groaning in pain. We three hugged each other tightly as she was shedding myriad amount of tears – like a small baby. For over five minutes, she kept crying – in pain, anguish. When she emptied all her tears and was sobbing atrociously, she looked up.

"Why Dhruv? Why me? I left the person who almost got himself killed without food for me. Why am I so cruel?" She squeaked. M held our hand tightly.

"Angie my friend, you are not cruel, you are just doing what is right at the moment. You are right! Even if Prasoon uncle is ready to leave the house, you can't let him…." And then she turned to me, taking my hand and giving me Angie's hand on the other hand, we three were holding each other's hands... and she continued, "Angie, this is not the end of your story; we will not let your love end like this. Mithu! Today's promise, I'm going to take in front of Angie. Promise me! You'll bring Ansh and Angie together again."

I did. I made the promise by holding Angie's hand, M's hand and I'm glad that I made it.

Later, much later, I learned that it was not me who brought them together. M, my smart ass girlfriend did it with all her intelligence. She was the one who planned an extraordinary end of their love story.

I'm sitting on my bed, thinking about my future with Dhruv, of which I'm completely oblivious of. Will he ever be able to move on? Or am I just running after a shadow who does not want to see the light? My pros and cons are constantly trying to manipulate me – playing with my emotions, increasing my confusion. Suddenly, my phone beeps – it's him. My jaw dropped when I read the text.

'Nilu! I know you are doing things for me which no one can ever dream of doing. Knowing my dark side, you still love me for who I am. In fact, I love you too…I really do. But when I think of us being together, a thought of cheating comes across my mind. I still love M and I love you too. I just can't understand the feelings I'm having inside. Is it possible to love two people at the same time? Well, I don't have an answer to that, but I need you. I need you beside me – holding my hand just like you have been doing for the past eight months. I need you; just don't leave me, ever. I can't afford to lose you again.'

I can hear my heart beating till my throat. My pros and cons have fainted – speechless and I know this is the time to tell him the truth that he deserves to know. I still can hear my heart as I dial his number.

"Hello!"

"Hey Nilu!"

"Oh my god Dhruv, you are drunk…Again!"

"Sorry Nilu, but I had to. You'll understand it once you read my mail."

"Just take care of yourself, Dhruv. Don't drink too much and call me tomorrow."

"Okay M, love you, bye."

That's it! He loves M. He doesn't have a place for me in his heart. My pros and cons are back, smirking at me. For the first time, they are on the same side – arching their brows at me. Why M, why? Why are you doing this to me, my friend?

I open my mailbox and start reading.

8 February

When I reached inside her room with the tray full of flowers and a note, she had her eyes opened and I was happy enough to ignore her flummox eyes. I put the envelope in her hand and leaned forward to kiss her. For the first time in those eight days, she moved her face away from me. I was standing discombobulate – snapping at her to check if she was doing it on purpose or not and she reared back. I then tried to reach her hand, but before I could hold on to it, she snatched it away from me. My head started burning, *what the hell was she up to?* I tried it again – by trying to take her in my arms and before my hands could reach her body, she screamed out,

"Who are you???" My heart chocked in my mouth as I heard her and she was loud – loud enough to make mom-dad run inside our room. They shed a few tears, but weren't as surprised as I was.

'Can anyone tell me what the hell is going on?'

"The time is near, Dhruv! Prepare yourself." That's all dad could say before leaving the room. Mom followed him. Then only I pressured my mind to look into the books I've read and almost forgotten. Peripheral nerve sheath tumour, they are eating her brain. Was it our time to part our ways? What was the point for me to be there when she couldn't even recognise me? It would make everything worse and painful for me. What about the promises? The story I was writing for her? Was everything going in vain? Didn't she remember any of them? The notes I had written for her? The orchids I gave? The kisses I marked on her lips? Had the tumour cells eradicated all of them from her memory? My mind was playing with my tears and me when I heard footsteps of mom and dad. Without saying a word, dad handed her two envelopes. They were of two different colours, one sky blue and one purple.

"Just leave her alone for some time, Dhruv!" Dad tapped my shoulder and I followed them out with tears in my eyes. I wasn't ready for this. I certainly wasn't.

I didn't have a choice, did I? She had taken her word from us about not calling her a doctor and I hate her for that. I still do. I then realised something about men. They feel a burning sensation inside their head, especially when they don't feel right or realise that things are not going their way, but can't do anything to change it. That's the most embarrassing part of human life.

"Everything will be fine, son!" Dad told me – whose consolation didn't affect me at the time.

"How dad? She has forgotten me. How can this be fine?" I squeaked in pain.

"This is temporary Dhruv! Besides, she knew this was coming and was prepared for this. Trust me, she'll be normal again. But, what I'm afraid of is that the time is near. One or two days if we are lucky!"

"What??? I'm not going to let this happen. Not this soon!" That's all I could say with all my challenging abilities. They sat quiet; they weren't surprised by my reaction. They knew, had it been the first death coming in this family, they would have acted the same way, but they'd seen it before, many times. How could God be so cruel to this lovely family? Things like these made me doubt god's existence in my mind.

But, not after what I heard...

"Mithu!" I rushed into our room as I heard it again – the voice, which I was craving to hear. As I went inside, I saw her blue eyes suspiciously checking me out.

"Sorry Mithu! I didn't know it would come this way," I still caught her eyes rolling at me as if she wasn't sure of my presence or may be... it was me.

"M! Are you sure you remember me?" I finally asked, staring straight into her eyes, searching for the truth. Her blue eyes – like cocker spaniel which had just messed on the rug.

"Okay, I admit, I don't. I mean yes, I do, but you'll have to help me with that. I knew it coming and made a few preparations myself, but they are not going to work without you holding my hand beside me. Understand?"

I didn't have the energy to separate my emotions; instead they were jumbled together, indistinguishable. I was standing pale, like an overloaded outlet, as if a breaker had tripped inside me, leaving me incapable of any action.

"Understand Mithu?" She reached for my hand by saying that.

"I could do it for the rest of my life." My answer was obvious and true.

"I know, but you are allowed to do it for the rest of *my* life, which is going to end soon!" Before I could break into tears, she pulled my head for a morning kiss. It was never quick and perfunctory, like acquaintances greeting each other. Our kisses were everlasting. I never pulled back and nor did she – the kiss lasted for a lifetime of its own. And when we finally drew apart, I knew with certainty that I'd done the right thing. It always was a blockbuster kiss. But that – with all exuberant affection – could not constrain our cheeks from getting wet. Two of us were crying while kissing; that was unlike us.

"It felt like the first kiss of my life," she said after we finished. Though it struck me hard on my chest, that innocent essence in her voice made me smile.

"You'll be getting plenty of these my love!" I said and squeezed her palm.

"I'm counting on that," and she blushed! My genius, impeccably beautiful blue-eyed girl was back.

Unlike Alzheimer, memory loss in Neurofibrosarcoma is flaccid and capricious. May be once in a day, week…depending on her rapidly growing tumour cells. But as dad told me, everyone in their family died within two days after getting the first stroke of memory loss. Two days? What about the Valentine's Day? We were supposed to celebrate it together.

'Please my lord! Convince my faith in you. Please let us celebrate this Valentine's Day together. I beg you please!'

"So what's in today's note?" She moved my thoughts with her sweet voice. I then reached out for the plate full of orchids and the envelope.

What if we never broke up?
What if we faced it together?
What if we had more time together?
What if I hadn't become an alcoholic?
So many "what ifs" and so many possibilities, which can never be changed.
But one can,
Since I haven't proposed you officially, can this propose day be our official patch up?

She gazed at me for long before she answered, "You cannot take that away from me!" And I – without any reservations – reached for her lips.

We kissed, a kiss as captivating as heaven itself. Eradicating all those "what ifs" from my mind, we thanked our God for the moment, with a selfish desire to give us a few more days before taking her away.

She spent her afternoon in revising the notebook, while I was busy in remembering all the time I spent with her, wondering – with this bloody disease – how much she remembered. There were only a few days left and I knew it well. So for her, concentrating on the past was trying to decipher an image on a fuzzy television screen. She couldn't remember one way or the other – no matter how hard she would try. All she could do was to live those memories through my words. That's when I realised the power of words. They can make you live those forgotten moments, a wonderful lifespan, which only a book can offer. The possession it takes over the soul is rare in comparison to films or any other form of story narration. I owe my words to M, after all she was the one who pulled this off. I'm just a conveyer.

At night, after having sweet corn soup cooked by mom and me, we both lay on our bed with the notebook in my hand. In a way, it was the first narration to her so we both were exited.

And I started reading.

On the way to Cafe Piano, Ansh was sitting sombrely, wanting to have no conversation at all. And Dhruv – knowing his friend regardless of any explanations – was giving him what he needed the most, silence-the only thing he could offer to his friend at the moment. Had he been in Ansh's shoes, he knew he wouldn't be as calm as Ansh was. He'd have smashed all the obstacles that would come between him and his love. At least that's what he believed then, not knowing that the obstacles were on their way and there was nothing he could do about it.

Once they reached there and faced Mr. Shah, both couldn't help but notice his red, swollen eyes. Dhruv and Ansh felt like someone has backed over them with a truck. Angie, who held a special position in their lives, felt cursed after seeing her father like that.

Without uttering a word, both took their respective seats.

"Hello sons!" Even with so much pain, Mr. Shah was kind enough to greet them with a smile, but boys being boys merely nodded.

"I guess Ansh, your girlfriend has already told you what happened yesterday," he continued, understanding and ignoring their despondence.

"Yes, sir! And you are not leaving the house, not for us," he ordained. Mr. Shah welcomed it with a smile.

"I expected this from you and that's why I called you. Forget about Angie; tell me, will you be able to see someone else after her?"

The question struck him hard inside, something that stirred everything inside of him, something sudden and unexpected. And before he could stop the words, they were out.

"No!" And tears started pricking his eyes, knowing that it was true. Somewhere between when he saw Angie for the first time and they made love for the first time, he'd learned that life without Angie was hopeless and meaningless. Even though he hadn't thought about it since last night, the very first thought irked by Mr. Shah frightened him. It was a nightmare he did not want to live.

"I know and you won't have to. Trust me."

"How, sir?" That's all he could say.

"Angel is twenty-one now. I've seen her growing up in front of my eyes. Since her childhood, she has been a "grown-up" kid. Usually, kids have their own needs. When they see various dolls and toys in fellow children's hands, an urge to have the same bubbles in them. But, she was different. She knew what things I could afford and what I couldn't. She never allowed herself to get fascinated by those luxuries I couldn't afford, but as a father you must know what your child needs. During her 'Athai Tap', for the first time she asked for something –

you! Now she thinks that she asked for too much and you are one of those luxuries which I cannot afford. But she is wrong. I can, and I will. And as I see you, I can say that I'm proud of my upbringing. She could not have asked for anything better than you. You are one good man Ansh and I promise I'll fix this. All I'm asking for is some time. Can you two give that to me?" Ansh nodded, with tears in his eyes – just like Mr. Shah. Dhruv, who was listening to the conversation all ears, cleared his throat,

"Of course, Mr. Shah! I know my friends Ansh and Angie and I know that breaking apart is the last thing they want from life. And we will not let them." He said firmly, meaning it. Ansh knew he did not need to say anything; all he needed to do was trust his best friend and a great man sitting in front of him.

After finishing his coffee, Mr. Shah asked for the cheque to which both Dhruv and Ansh refused as they were going to have their lunch there. Mr. Shah hugged both of them and left.

"Accident!" The doorkeeper screamed and ran out. Ansh and Dhruv didn't want to hear it, as they already had a thunderstorm to deal with.

After five minutes, the manager ran inside and reached towards them.

"Excuse me, sir! I think he's the gentleman who was sitting with you earlier, who met with an accident."

"What???" Ansh squeaked and ran out. Dhruv followed him.

They saw Mr. Shah on the ground, full of blood and wounded, his tibial bone was broken and displaced. He was partially conscious, which undoubtedly was a good sign. He was shaking his hands in pain.

"Please call 108 Gajju!" Ansh cried out.

Dhruv somehow was able to compose himself.

"Calm down, Ansh. 108 will take minimum ten-fifteen minutes to come. Let me call Bhai. I think he is somewhere nearby."

He immediately took out his phone and called his brother.

"Where are you Bhai?"

"At my friend's hospital, what happened?"

"Is it nearby SG road? Angie's father had an accident; we are at the Cafe Piano-TGB."

"Shit! Listen, don't panic and drive him here. Make sure he remains conscious. I'm texting you the address. It's just five minutes away from there."

"Okay Bhai! Coming!"

He ended the call and turned to Ansh.

"Ansh! Go and get my car from basement," he threw the car keys at Ansh which he took and ran away.

"Excuse me, sir!" A voice came from behind. Dhruv turned around and saw the doorkeeper standing. "This is the number of that Audi car. The entire accident might have been caught in front door's CCTV as well."

Dhruv thanked him for that but at that time Mr. Shah's treatment was the first concern for them. Ansh drove the car near to where Dhruv and Mr. Shah were and was quick in opening the back door. Dhruv lifted Mr. Shah and placed him in the backseat, while Ansh remained on the driving paddle. Within five minutes, they reached the given address and saw Dhruv's brother standing at the gate with a stretcher held by other doctors and nurses. They took charge as he lifted him out and put him on the stretcher. They drew Mr. Shah inside while Dr. Brijesh was standing, helping them to clean up the blood in the backseat.

"How did it occur?" Dr. Brijesh asked.

"An Audi hit him on the service road. I guess whoever was on the driver's seat, was completely drunk." Dhruv shrugged his shoulder, a wave of nausea sweeping through his head.

"Okay. I'll have to inform the police first," he said and pulled out his phone, but before he could dial the number, Dhruv interfered.

"This is the car number and accident is recorded in the front camera of TGB. And Bhai…"

"What Dhruv?"

"That bastard must not get away."

"He will not. Don't worry." His brother ensured him.

Angie and her family arrived at the hospital within an hour.

"Where is he?" Her mother – whose eyes were still wet and widened by shock – asked.

"Inside, let's go!" Dhruv answered and led them inside.

When they reached inside, they saw a lower extremity cast on his right foot. Mr. Shah was still unconscious. Dhruv started observing everyone's faces. Angie and her mother were weeping, their eyes moistened and swollen. The rest were just standing quietly. Angie's Badepapa was looking at him with ignominy. Only then did Dhruv realise that he wasn't enjoying Dhruv's leadership for sure. Dhruv somehow ignored him and saw some police officers coming.

"Where is Dr. Brijesh Gajjar?" The inspector asked.

"Just a moment, sir!" Dhruv said and asked a nurse to call his brother.

He came out and shook hands with the inspector.

"Here are the detailed reports of the patient, inspector! His name is Prasoon Shah and this is his family. You can get further details from them and any progress on the accused driver?"

"Yes, Dr. Gajjar! He was arrested at Thaltej Circle where he got involved in another accident. His name is Vishal Shah, son of the famous businessman, Akhilesh Shah. He was completely drunk while driving."

"Excuse me? Did you say Akhilesh shah?" Angie's Badepapa emerged from nowhere.

"Yes, who are you?" The inspector asked. He didn't like to get interrupted.

"I'm Prasoon's elder brother." He answered and looked at Dhruv with an unspoken indication.

"Yes, do you know them?"

"Very well. He is the most reputed person of our community."

"We all know about his reputation. He is nothing but just a goon with lots of money," the inspector snapped at him.

"Whoever he is, file the strongest charge sheet against him inspector!" Dr. Brijesh said.

'And that's why he is my big B. Proud of you brother!' Dhruv kept his words to himself.

"We do not want any complaint against him from our side," Angie's Badepapa said. Everyone, even the inspector was stunned by his response.

"What? You want to let the person who almost killed your brother walk free?" Dr. Brijesh groaned.

"My brother is alive. So we do not want any complaints."

"He is alive because we brought him here in time," Dhruv growled at him with anger.

"And I thank you for that, but our decision is final. We don't want to file any complaint." He said with folded hands and clenched teeth.

"Let me tell you something, whatever you are doing is not going to help him much. He was caught drunk. So he is going to jail anyway," the inspector said and it somehow pleased Dhruv.

"Excuse me inspector, I need to go to another hospital. I'll be in touch with you for further updates." Dhruv could sense some disappointment in his brother's voice, as he also had his limitations as a doctor.

"Okay, Dr. Gajjar. We are also leaving. I think we are done with this case." The inspector said and snapped at Angie's Badepapa again before leaving.

Dhruv again gazed at everyone. Angie's mother and Angie were crying, just crying. Her Badepapa and Rishi were still giving him that ignominious look. Ansh was standing too, but still as a rock with a frowned face. Everything seemed to play with his emotions – first disbelief, then grief and finally anger.

"Guys, you are going to succumb to these bastards? You are going to sacrifice each other for people like them?" Dhruv groaned.

Ansh and Angie looked up in shock, unable to find any words. Angie's cousin Rishi got closer to him.

"Don't you dare to talk about my father like that!"

"What would you do? And tell me what can you do? Look at me, I'm not Anshul Bhatt. I'm Dhruv Gajjar and you don't know what I can make out of you. I have been teaching lessons to losers of your kind since very long and believe me, I'm best at it." Dhruv clenched his fists and shot at him with his eyes. His father probably noticed Dhruv's red ears and burning face. He knew if he and his son got involved in a duel, his son did not stand a chance. He too came forward.

"Rishi, let's go. We will meet my brother after his discharge. We don't need to deal with these goons. And Angel, if you still want to be with this boy, then prepare yourself along with your father to leave our house." Both walked out of the hospital tapping their feet in anger. Dhruv stared at Ansh who was staring at Angie. Perhaps he was expecting her to say something. Actually they both were. But all they could see was a girl crying voraciously on her mother's shoulder.

"Seems like you both have given up, but I won't. They will have to pay for this and I'll make them," Dhruv scoffed.

"This is none of your business, Gajju! You should stay in your limits," Ansh said. The words hit him with a great physical force. He felt breathless, unable to feel his body and a riot of warring thoughts and overwhelming anger filled his mind.

"Excuse me! Are you talking to me? And what the fuck is this limitation thing?"

Ansh made an abortive attempt to calm Dhruv by putting his hand on his shoulder, which Dhruv deflected and pushed away before he could reach. Ansh ignored it and continued, "We must understand each other's limitations, Gajju! This is neither your family matter nor mine. We all should leave them alone. Can't you see that she doesn't want us? Can't you see that she doesn't even consider our help? And apart from that, we are friends, not each other's guardians. You are not my father who can protect me from this bad world." Dhruv wasn't convinced by any of his words. He was blindfolded with his anger.

"From now on, you two better stay away from me." He said before walking out.

She was looking at me with a stunned face when I finished. I reached for her hand and gently placed it on my lap.

"Pretty messy it went," she said.

"Yeah, it did!"

"You didn't mention me anywhere today."

"Tomorrow, I'll tell you how we broke up."

"Oh, was it hard to get through?"

"Yes, it took our seven months away from each other."

"Oh, well, then I hope I see tomorrow!"

Tears started pricking my eyes as her words punched me hard in my gut.

"You will. Trust me,"

She then picked up the envelopes and started reading something from them. I wanted to see what's inside, but I wasn't allowed to. *'May be when she sleeps,'* I thought, but didn't know what was coming.

"It says I have to take a promise from you now," she softly said.

"I know, go on!" I again bowed my head.

"Promise me! You'll never touch these envelopes even after my death."

"I promise!"

And those colourful envelopes remain an unsolved mystery to me. Even today.

Before I start reading the next part Dhruv sent me, I seek an answer from you. What if you've a secret inside which probably can change your life? Which could either be exuberant or malicious? I don't know if the secret I'm keeping inside of me will bring happiness or loneliness for me, but all I know is that Dhruv is not the only one who's keeping the promises; I too am. And what I wonder is whether I will ever be able to share it with him or not. Will I ever get the courage to share it with him? What would be his reaction after that? Will he be willing to see me again after that?

May be…May be not…

Had it been seven years back, I would know exactly what he would say, how he would react. But now he is an entirely different person – the person who's my best friend but also a person who does not see his future with me.

Or maybe he just needs some time, and I won't mind waiting for him for the rest of my life. Or maybe I would. A thought does nothing romantic except making me dreadful. Fear is a strong emotion – having the ability to conquer trust, affection and sensibility, and to replace them with anger, hurt and bitterness.

The answer I seek from you is, should we keep a secret from someone we love or not? Even if it can break everything that belongs to you?

Perhaps I'm not responsible for it; perhaps I'm.

But not more than my friend…M, where are you? I need your help and I'm coming to talk to you.

9 February

I was placing M's favourite white chocolates on the wooden tray along with some orchids. Mom who was standing there, couldn't help but smile. We all had our eyes swollen red. They, along with me, had been crying all night long. We even prayed for some miracle to happen. Can miracles happen in real life? When was the last time I felt something miraculous?

The answer was obvious and easy – when I saw her blue eyes for the first time. Unlike her, her mom had grey eyes, like a Greek goddess. She too, like M, is blessed with mesmerizing beauty and grace.

I swung the door and saw her sitting on her bed with the envelopes.

What? She forgot everything again? That punched me hard in the stomach. I somehow couldn't convince myself with the fact that it was never going to be the same between us, as it was before. I was standing dumbstruck with her snapping at me. I chose to refrain myself from saying a word. After a brief silence, she softly spoke.

"Are you Dhruv?"

"Yes, ma'am, I am!"

"Are you sure? I mean, you didn't con me into something, did you? I can't see any reason for you deserving to be my boyfriend."

I frowned, stared at my toes, embarrassed.

"Sorry for that!"

"Did we have sex? I mean, did you ever get your filthy fat body on me?"

"No M, I didn't…get my filthy hands on you."

"I knew it. I would never allow a fat pig like you to touch me."

I swallowed, unsure of what to say. After all, the person sitting in front of me wasn't my girlfriend. My M knew me to the core of my soul and I didn't blame her for forgetting me. Even if I'd been a hundred times fatter than I was before, she would still love me like she did. Once you ascertain love, everything else seems minuscule in front of it.

"I know M, and you didn't. Don't worry!" I softly answered.

"Now get lost, I don't want to see your shitty face."

This was it. The magical moments we spent for the past eight days had come to an end. This part of her didn't want me with her. I gently placed the plate beside her and reached for the door. To see my blue-eyed girl for the last time, I turned around and saw her laughing.

"GOTCHYA!" She screamed. And I sighed audibly and rushed to her.

"You almost killed me, bitch!"

"Just bitch?"

"Okay, sexy bitch!"

"Just sexy bitch?"

"My sexy bitch. Okay?"

"Fair enough!"

And we bumped our heads in laughter, but not before putting her favourite white chocolates in my mouth and sliding it into her mouth from mine. Her tongue and lips felt tastier than ever; perhaps the prank she played had its effect on it.

She then, as a ritual, kissed the orchids and opened the envelope.

Today – since you don't remember most of the time we spent together – I will tell you about a moment related to this white chocolate.

One day, we had a belligerent fight over some issues, and you – holding your anger on your about-to-turn-red nose – didn't want to see my face. For about ten long days, you kept your head burning and rejected all my apologies. On the eleventh day, you agreed to meet me. We talked about nothing that day; neither had you apologised, nor had I. We just sat there and ate those white chocolates I had brought for you. When we finished and I stood up to leave – with no hope of reconciliation – I softly asked you, "Shall we meet again?"

And, of course with a smile, your answer was, "Only if you bring me these chocolates."And I rushed towards you and took you in my arms. For the following ten days, we met and without sharing a word, ate these chocolates – while holding each other's hand.

She giggled while putting the note down, blessed my lips with the morning kiss and softly said, "You have been a great lover Mithu! And I remember that. Even death cannot make me forget your 'no apologies' attitude."

I laughed, because that was true…I've been egoistic at times.

On the ninth day after dinner – in which she had our favourite paneer, unlike regular soups – we sat on the bed. The hardest part of the narration was on its way and we both knew it.

And so I started reading.

Dhruv woke up, half sleep when he heard his phone ringing.

"Hello Dhruv? You there?" Spoke Mr. Shah, over the phone.

"Yes, Mr. Shah! How's your leg?"

"Listen to me carefully. Angel and Ansh are together right now. I forced Angie to meet him. Rishi heard this conversation. I saw him and around ten of his friends going out with bats and hockey sticks in their hands," Dhruv could clearly sense a certain fear in his voice.

'This is serious and above our differences. Move your ass Gajju!'

"Where are they?" He asked while getting his car keys.

"At Shambhu's coffee-bar."

"Okay, Mr. Shah! Don't worry, I'm on my way."

He hung up the phone, walked out and sat in his car. Shambhu's coffee bar was probably twenty minutes away from his house, but on that day it took him merely five to seven minutes to reach there. Obviously by troubling people on the road and by changing lanes swiftly.

As he reached, he saw Ansh and Angie inside through the glass door, with fear in their eyes. Rishi and the gang were waiting for them outside. The security guard was holding his rifle more tightly than ever to avoid any trouble inside the coffee bar. Ansh and Angie were not coming out because they knew that they were safe as long as they were inside, but they could not stay there forever. Dhruv walked towards Rishi.

"You better stay out of this," Rishi stared at him with anger.

"Do you think I'm going to?" He replied and moved closer to him.

"Do you think you are going to beat all of us with your tiny muscles?" He retorted.

"Thanks for reminding that I'm outnumbered and I know I actually am. But, I don't care. Because I'm not going to fight you all! I'm just going to keep all my attention on one person and whoever he will be; I'll beat him till death. May be, I'll die in the process, maybe I even survive…which I know I will. So if you still want to try then tell me, who's coming first? You or some of your punter?" He said, moving even closer – head to head. He was showing courage not because he was brave, but because he had to. It was a risk that he had to take for the people he loved the most.

"She must come back home within an hour," Rishi ordered and cringed.

Dhruv realised that the plan had worked; he did not have to fight them.

"She will come back, whenever she would feel like coming, and remember, if you ever try to repeat anything like this again, then you and your punters will not reach home on your legs. I can promise you that," Dhruv's confidence was on a high node.

"I will see you." He said while walking away.

"You are seeing me right now, this is who I am. If you want to see me again, then just call me. But right now, why don't we play a game which is called "fuck-off" and you go first!" Dhruv sighed. As they all left the place, he started walking his car. Angie and Ansh came closer to him.

"Gajju!" Ansh called him.

"Don't you dare to call me Gajju, only my friends do that and you two lost me a while ago."

"Dhruv, please try to understand..." Angie started saying but chocked in her sobs.

"Please Angie! I don't want to be rude to a girl, just back off. You know the person you refused to take a stand for last night, called me to save your asses. That man still cares for you. Your father, he called me. Shame on you two for not having a little courage to stand for what is right." He growled, sat in his car and drove away.

Dhruv didn't head to his home after that; he instead went to meet M who had already reached there before him. It had been nearly over two months after Mr. Shah's accident that they met each other, so Dhruv was excited to see his blue-eyed girl where on the other hand, somehow, M was frightened with what was coming. As most staff members already knew her, they were astounded with the way she reached there.

When Dhruv entered, the only thing he saw was M sitting there. Sad and in tears, which he thought were because of Ansh and Angie.

"Don't cry for those losers, M! They are not worth it," Dhruv said and held her hand. She immediately took it back, which stunned Dhruv more than it hurt him.

"The problem is not with them, Dhruv! It's about us!"

Dhruv gazed at her blue eyes to figure out what she was hiding beneath them.

"What are you talking about M?" He said.

"It's not working Dhruv! Between us…"

That punched him hard in his stomach, but he didn't say a word. He still believed that M was playing a game with him.

"You're not serious… Are you?" He paused.

"I am, Dhruv, we seriously need to think…"

"That's not what I meant. I meant about us, you were really never serious about us, right?"

Underneath his anger, he perhaps wanted her to say no. He wanted her to say she didn't mean what she said earlier. To his astonishment, she didn't say a word and perhaps that made him angrier, even cruel.

"Answer me, M!" She didn't answer and he continued.

"You used me. You wanted a boyfriend who'd spend bucks for your expenses. You never were serious about us, right?" In his heart, Dhruv was praying that she would slap him on his face and tell him that it's all a lie. She loves him till eternity and this would mean nothing at all. But contrary to that, she looked away. Dhruv, who was already high on anger, now stood up and punched the table hard which forced the other costumers' and restaurant staff's attention towards him.

The manager who was in his fifties and knew them closely – was witnessing everything from a side. As knew something like this was going to happen, he'd already told all the staff members not to intervene.

"You've seen the best side of me so far M! Now you'll see the worst and I promise M, you'll regret it more than me."

And he walked out, stamping his feet on the floor.

After he left, M burst into tears. Her dad came and sat beside her. When she'd shed every drop, her father along with the manager – who too was in tears – put her on her wheelchair.

Before she left the restaurant, the manager said with his hand on M's head, "I'll pray for you my child!"

"It's too late for that uncle! It's too late for that…"

She mumbled before leaving.

I groaned in tears as I finished the last line I did what I couldn't do the last time, cried hard in pain, grief, sorrow. She took me in her arms and started rubbing my back with her hand. I broke into tears; the part I knew I would have to narrate disheartened had finally arrived. And ironically, crying was the only thing I could do – or perhaps I was allowed to do.

"Mithu…Mithu… Calm down baby!" She rubbed my back with both of her hands when I collapsed in her arms and broke down.

When tears stopped falling, I was sitting quietly, holding her hand.

"Who told you about what happened after you left?" She softly asked.

"Dad," I murmured.

"Of course he did!" She squeezed my hand hard and kissed me on my wet cheek. At that time her lips felt soothing.

I knew it was now the promise time and I was getting ready for it. And she said, "Promise me! You'll try to learn patience. You'll not let my death go in vain. You'll come out of it as a better person."

"I promise I'll try, my love! You know it's not in my hands."

She laughed at this and kissed me on my neck before blessing my lips.

And we slept together, in smile together, in tears together, in love together.

After having a conversation with M in solitude, I'm feeling relieved and strong. It may look unrealistic and confusing to you, but that's the way it is. We all have secrets within us and believe me, M also stands for mystery; A genius intellectual who will blow your mind soon. Trust me.

I stand up and push the handle to open the door. Being with her in that room always gives me the strength I require – knowing that this is the same room where Dhruv wrote his entire story and narrated to her. Can I be envious of it? No, not at all – may be a little but not enough to affect my friendship with M. Outside the room, on the sofa, her dad and mom are sitting. I hug them both as soon as I meet them.

"How's Dhruv?" Dad asks. Since they can't talk to each other, I'm the messenger who's been telling them about the overall improvement in Dhruv.

I do not reply. Instead, I pull out my phone and show him his recent picture. His mouth wears a happy smile as soon as he sees it. His could-have-been-son-in-law looks much younger, fitter than the last time he saw him. He'd lost about ten kilos and yet was not stopping. He gently takes it from my hand and shows it to M's mom. The same smile emerges on her face too.

"This is the boy who my daughter chose to date." She quipped.

"A correction my dear, daughters…" No wonder where M got a great sense of humour from. I couldn't help but smile shyly in front of them.

Only then I received a text from Dhruv saying, 'I've sent you a mail. It has a part of my life you need to know the most. I don't have any explanations or excuses for what I became, but I promised her and now I promise you too that no matter how hard life becomes, I won't be like that again. Ever.'

A sudden twitch of fear rises within my flesh. I finally will get to know what and how hard it was. What has he done to think that he doesn't deserve me! What's there that keeps haunting him?

10 February

It was hard to wake up every day; answers started coming out in mumbles and words were able to make their way out with great effort. There was no hair left on her head, leaving it almost bald. To be honest, in one corner of my heart, I started hating being there. There's nothing more painful than seeing your loved one like, especially when you are not allowed to do anything about it.

She said that we were having a chance to say goodbye. But was it something I really wanted? Or needed? Certainly not wanted, but needed? Well, she knew me better.

She was getting weaker with time. But I somehow hoped that she'd survive till the Valentine's Day. At least Valentine's Day! She was weak enough not to bother to see the orchids, and the note I wrote, I had to read it out to her.

Mistakes are happenstance,
Some make few, some more,
But they are solely responsible for their mistakes,
Just as I'm responsible for all of mine,

Today, I shall be the one seeking a promise from you,
Promise me! You won't blame yourself for all the mistakes I've made.

A drop of tear emerged on her left eye, making its way to her radiating cheeks, calling me to lick every bit of it. And – as it was my first duty – I accomplished it by licking all of the salt that fell from her eyes.

"I promi…" It took her a while to coax those words out.

That day went quietly. As we both knew we needed some moments of silence before what was coming to us, and for the first time, the birds on the outside were chattering more than the birds inside. Mom and Dad had also anticipated that the time of her departure was near and they seemed burdened by the truth, while I was still hoping for a miracle, which I knew was not going to come.

And for the first time, I was having tears in my eyes the moment I started reading.

She was gone, and Dhruv too made no attempts to make any amends. Days turned into weeks, weeks turned into months and it was already over six months since Dhruv and M broke up. On the day his parents received his detention letter. He started thinking about his life in the past tense, for all that had happened in the past six months. As he was true to his words, he did not leave a single chance to corrupt himself physically, mentally and morally. The detention letter was sent to his home for not attending a single day in college for six months and also not participating in the final exams. He'd have to repeat the entire year. None of his family members knew of it until the letter reached their hands. Dhruv neither offered any explanation for doing this, nor bothered to talk to them. Just a text was sent to his brother from his side that he was coming over.

On the way to his home, he tried to remember how the past six months had gone. The first thing he lost after his breakup was his friends. He fought with everyone who he considered his friend. Ansh was living in a hostel with his friends and Dhruv – just as he wanted – did everything possible to make sure he ruins his life. Cigarettes and weeds, that had been his sworn enemies, turned into his life partners. Alcohol took the place of protein shakes. A couple of nightstands with girls he'd never entertained. His muscles were gone and there were now thirty extra kilos and an eight-inch increment to his waist.

His seat belt was now feeling tighter than ever. He wasn't bothering to check the speed he was on. All he was thinking about was how blessed his life had been and how he had ruined it completely. He thought about how he fell in love with M and what made them go apart. He tried to think about that a lot in those six months, but never really got an answer and that's why it started getting worse day by day. He thought about all the mistakes he made, all the trust and faith he broke, all the dreams he shattered. He wasn't drunk, but wasn't fine either. Had it been six months ago, he'd have kept his eyes on the road but on that day, he didn't. He didn't realise when his car started heading towards the left side, not that he wasn't aware about the consequences of over-speeding. He knew he made a mistake and his car was losing control. There was a time when he could've controlled it, but he didn't. He let the wheels do their job and he was ready to embrace death. He felt his car flipping a couple of times, he felt the airbags breaking out and he also felt the light of death coming towards him. He was ready to die, he had his moments of happiness – fortunately more than anyone else he knew – he had his moments of love, moments of completeness, also the moments of pain, infidelity and anguish. He truly was ready to die.

But he survived.

The next thing he remembered was waking up on his bed and seeing Ansh sitting beside him. His mom and sister-in-law on the right side – in tears. And his father, brother standing with their eyes arching a thousand questions.

There were a lot of questions to be asked and he never really had their answers. Answers he was trying to find from the past six months. Was it some kind of revenge? From whom? For whom? A girl whom he met two years ago? He imagined the answer, he jeopardised his career and ruined his entire life because of a girl, who for him didn't even exist two years ago! No, he scraped off the thought straight away.

For over a month, he was grounded. His family was worried – angry too, having answers-seeking eyes arched at him. But Ansh requested them not to question him much. He ensured them that he'll personally look after Dhruv and make sure that he gets back on the right track. His family trusted Ansh and perhaps fortunately more than Dhruv, so no more questions were asked.

After a month, Ansh asked Dhruv's parents to take him out, to which they agreed – on a condition that he'll be on the driving wheels. His car was back, back from the dead. Luckily, there was an insurance to be used, so Dhruv was sure he'd not get bashed for money loss. He rose and felt his legs; they were working, unharmed. He was lucky, lucky enough to survive the accident with just a scratch on his right eyebrow. The airbags and the seat belt did their job fantastically; he couldn't forget to thank the Volkswagen engineering for making such a safety-featured car.

After Ansh ignited the engine, Dhruv asked, "Where are we going?"

"To M's house."

Dhruv snapped at him, with grief and anger.

"I don't want to meet that bitch Ansh!"

"Mind your words Gajju! She isn't a bitch; you need to know something."

And Dhruv crumbled on his knees as he saw her, almost bald and dying.

"That's it?"

"Yes, my love! That was our story." I took her hand and placed the diary on it.

"It feels incomplete…"she mumbled.

"That's the way it is," I wryly answered, putting a smile on her lovely face, which worked.

"It's still great."

"Yes, that it is!"

"And romantic too!"

"Yes, because of you…"

"I take that with grace."

And we kissed. With that kiss I remembered everything, the moment I saw her blue eyes, the moment I kissed her hand, cheeks, head and lips for the first time. Each and every moment – like a complete romantic film – presented itself before my mind and of course, the pain of heartbreak, which seemed too minuscule compared to what it was now. And the fact that she was dying; the fact that she chose death over me. You can't hold your thoughts from coming, can you?

I was positioned attentively, knowing that it was now the promise time.

"Go on, my love!"

She took the envelope, unfolded it and pulled out a white paper and stared at it for a while.

"You don't need the promise which is written in it."

"What's it about?"

"Abandoning the weeds and all the other stuff, with which you puffed away and corrupted your amazing physique."

I smiled at her.

"I promise ma'am. Wait, does it include alcohol?"

"Nope, I don't want to take all of your fun away with me. You know your limits in that better than me. At least for now!" She winked, referring to some erotic memories.

"I suddenly need a drink now, want to see those sexy legs."

In no time, she uncovered it from the blanket – pale, black, mortified.

"They are no more." And she coaxed out a drop of tear from my eye. Seeing her losing her life was killing me too.

"Anyways, I promise!" I said and looked down.

Without wasting a word, we hugged and slept in each other's arms.

Sangeet night is over, everyone is heading home and we are at Ansh and Angie's house. Yes, they live together and there's a long story behind it. It's better if you read it from Dhruv's perspective. Their parents are already asleep and Dhruv and Ansh are dealing with flowers and gifts while Angie and I are making some coffee for them. Tomorrow is the big day, their wedding, and Angie looks enthusiastic and skittish at the same time. They are going to Singapore on their honeymoon and she's shying away from revealing more truth. Instead, she's pestering me to reveal something about my relationship with Dhruv, but as you all know, there's nothing to say. We haven't taken a single step further.

"Here you go, black dark espresso without milk. Just the way your boyfriend likes," Angie quips and turns off the machine.

"I don't know how he drinks it. I can't even take its smell."

"This is something you'll have to cope up with. Trust me; he loves it more than anything in this world."

"Wrong dear. M! He loves her more than anything else in this world," I say and she pauses for a while; she's missing her best friend, clearly, I can see that.

There's nothing in this world that can take M's place – not even me.

"He has to move on Nilu! And you must help him get over it," she suggests, unaware of my efforts which leads to nothing but confusions and fights.

"He doesn't want to. He loves her, and will, for the rest of his life. I can't see anyone else taking her place for him – especially me."

"He will, trust me dear, he will. And you don't need to take her place. You need to make your own,"

"You're right Angie, and that's what I'm trying to do. But, he doesn't have a place in his heart for anyone else, and I know that too!"

"No, he has. I know the way he looks at you. I don't know what's restraining him from approaching you, but I know he has feelings for you. And whatever I know of him, all I can say is that you're the only one who can be with him."

"I know what's restraining him. There are two reasons: One is the guilt of betrayal. He still feels he's cheating on M when he gives a thought about moving on. And another thing is that he thinks he doesn't deserve me. He has never said that to me or anyone, but that's what he feels. For the sake of mistakes he has done, he's cynical about us."

"And that's where we'll have to work together," she winks.

We head for their room where Ansh and Dhruv are sitting on the sofa. I hand him the coffee mug and sit beside Angie. I won't lie about the sensation I feel when his fingers touch mine. I couldn't help but smile sheepishly.

"Mmm, the only companion who's bearing my stress apart from you. Love it." He rolls his eyes at me. What does he mean by that?

"Stop hitting on my friend, Dhruv!" Angie sneers, arching her brow at him.

"I guess I'm allowed to, Nilu?"

What do I answer to that? I mean, yes, I want him, but, okay, he is allowed, that's all, I just nod.

"See Angie, whose friend is she?"

"I know, and that's why you're taking her for granted," Angie retorts, with a grin, and Dhruv along with Ansh, looks dumbfounded. I know what he's going to do now, he'll cut off the conversation. Wait…

"I don't think I take my friends for granted, Angie!" See, I told you. I'm friend-zoned, again.

"Dhruv, you remember when Ansh and I were scared of admitting our feelings and you used to pester us? You helped us and we thank you for that. But right now, when we're trying to help you, you're the one who's running away, and that's not the Dhruv Gajjar who has been my best buddy for five-and-a-half years." Angie stares at him, straight into his eyes, something which I can't do – until now.

"I agree with her, Gajju! I think it's been a year now. And what you're doing is too much," Ansh says.

Dhruv remains quiet for a while and so do I.

"What do you guys expect me to do?" he asks, crossing his arms together and bending his head down.

"Take a walk, like M suggested us to," Angie answers with a smile. I don't know how he's going to react. Any mention of M has either brought tears in his eyes or a long stroke of memories. I'm prepared for any, but contrary to that, he smiles. Thank god!

"Hmm, if the three of you permit, I want to say something to Nilu. May I?" He asks, my heart is in my mouth, what'd that be? Just another beating around the bush or something – of which I've been praying for so long – about us?

"Without any reservations…" Angie simpers and I shiver.

After a brief smile, he starts.

"Nilu, first of all, I need you to know something. My feelings for you are not just limited to friendship, it's much beyond that – one step away from love, and that's not because you're not good enough. You've been more than anything I could ever ask for…"

He pauses and I continue shivering. For the first time, I'm hearing those kind of words from him.

And he continues.

"But guys, you all know what we all have been through. Angie, your best friend M, you know what she means to us? Ansh, you know you owe her every slice of happiness you're having." They both nod, that's something you'll get to know about her later.

"And Nilu, I still love her and you know that better than anyone else. I'm afraid, afraid of not doing justice to you despite of the feelings I have for you. That's one thing, and besides that I've made mistakes…mistakes that drastically changed my life. I'm still trying to recuperate myself from that and I sincerely believe that you deserve someone better than me. I know you won't agree with me on that but that's because you love me and I'm aware of the feelings you have for me. Trust me Nilu, we're almost on the same page. But, as you all know I'm carrying a burden of my haunted past with me and that's too heavy for me…"

He moves closer, takes my right hand and my God, I flush.

"This is the hand which held me in my hardest times, this is the hand that has seen my worst and my best from the past fifteen years, and this is the hand I don't want to hurt with the disparity of my own mind. Tell me, would my best friend inside you forgive me if I hurt that girl who's madly in love with me?"

What do I say to this? I realise that more than anything else, he's my best friend. And he needs me, whether we go further from that or not. I shouldn't leave his hand. His hand, how can I undermine the copulative spark it gives me? But, when it comes to friendship, everything else is minuscule and shallow. I caress his head with my hand and touch his cheek with my thumb to wipe the tears he's shedding.

"Dhruv, you remember back in school when you had to stay away from me because Ansh didn't like me? What did I tell you? I had said, our friendship is above everything else and even if we can't be together forever, you'd still be the most important person in my life. I was twelve when I said this. I meant it then and I mean it now. Regardless of where life takes us, you'll continue to be the most important person in my life,"

And he breaks down in my arms, we both are in tears. A part of us is shedding tears for the intact and unbreakable friendship we share, and a part of us is shedding tears for the pain that came after remembering the person we both love – M! Yes, none of them know how much I love her and I'm completely unsure of what their reaction would be if I share that truth with them. I can't right now. I can't ruin the moment, not in-between the heavenly hug of the person I love. Because I'm wearing a traditional choli, I feel his hand on my half bare back, and oh my…I flush. Angie notices it and clears her throat, and we – unwillingly – drift apart.

"By the way Nilu, is there any chance of you forgiving me for those insane childhood stuffs? Your lines were touchy, but it was ironic when you drew me into that!" Ansh chuckles, trying to lighten things up.

"I do forgive you Ansh, as long as you obey every single rule of your to-be-wife." I retort with a grin. Angie throws a wry smile. Having friends is great; thank you, M!

After a brief chattering session, we are positioned to hear Dhruv and as I know, he's going to read us what he considers the worst part of his life. He's scared and is in tears already. We together hold his hand tight.

"Go on Gajju, you can do it," Ansh says.

"Are you guys sure? I mean it's your big day tomorrow. We shouldn't ruin the moment."

"Do it Dhruv; nothing's going to be ruined. We are with you, holding your hand, providing the courage you require."Angie utters. As you all know already, there's something terrible on its way, something that could shatter all the romance passing through your veins and turn it into anguish, grief and anger. Go only if you've the courage to do so, otherwise save it for tomorrow.

11 February

February 11, apparently the worst day of my life. I don't have any blissful memory of that day, although there must be some. I don't remember any, because of the promise she took from me. Those eleven days, more than anything, were a journey of love, pain, care, parenthood, friendship; in one word, a whole new life. I found my new self of which I'd been oblivious all my life. Sometimes you evolve being a completely different person than what you've thought of yourself.

I was, in fact, a nerd for whom how to survive detention due to lack of attendance was the only big problem. Another one would be how to arrange booze for the weekend party, or on a serious note, how to pass the semester exams. But, in those days, unwillingly, I had several encounters with various emotions. Having said that, the first thing that'd fill the list was loss. How can you imagine losing someone you love in your twenties? Had I known it before, I'd have choreographed some of the greatest moments for M, like the vacation she wanted to spend in Ireland; and then physical intimacy, we were never those types of people who consider premarital sex a sin, we just wanted to take some time – like we did before committing ourselves to each other – just to make it more exciting, oblivious to what the affliction destiny had planned for us!

Then I saw her, succumbing herself to death. I felt like dying too – like a tree withering without its roots, but there were two people who held my hand. They became my crying shoulders, my pillars of strength, M's parents – my mom and dad!

While my biological parents were completely oblivious of the twister whirling my life, they successfully filled my parents' shoes. In those two years of my relationship, I met them hardly once or twice, that too without much interaction. On the very first day, the amount of love her dad showered on me and the confidence with which he adopted me regardless of what I'd been…that was something magical. They had a small yet great family; a gorgeous daughter, a sweet mother and a proud father. They both were cardiologists, so they knew the routes of heart better than anyone else. Yes, they too were doctors and with all their resources, they couldn't save their only daughter. These are not my words; they said it and they'll blame themselves all their life for it.

In those twelve days, dad taught me patience, integrity and morality. How sometimes it is important to do something beyond traditions and rituals! He set a perfect example of true love. While mom – just like any other mom – had only one thing to offer, her unconditional affection and care. She taught me recipes of various soups, dishes and the biggest recipe – of hiding tears. She was always crying, but her face never showed that. Not because of anything else, but me; she knew that it was me who needed her more than she needed me. In those days, I grew up all over again, with the love of my life. In spite of a myriad amount of pain and grief, those days managed to create our little world, comprising happiness and joy – happiness of being together and the joy of learning various new things from them.

During those days, I made up my mind of looking after them once she is gone. I'll be their pillar of strength; I'll be their stick with whom they can grow old together. Not only for M, but for me too! And I wanted to make it a mission of my life, and I would've done it successfully if…

If that promise didn't come along.

"Promise me! You will never talk to my parents after my death."

"What? This is not done! I'm not giving any of those silly promises!" I snarled in frustration and I was loud, loud enough to drive mom-dad into our room.

When they learned what that was all about – to all my surprise – they stood silent.

"They've also given me their word Mithu! Please…" She mumbled, unable to finish her line. I glanced at them, they were clearly disappointed. But just like me, helpless too!

"Just give her what she wants and come in my room Dhruv. Let's have a drink together." Dad said and walked out; mom followed him without uttering a word.

I waited for a while for M to respond, but she didn't. I wanted to fight her on that – like those days when we didn't talk to each other for days – but, I didn't have those days. From where I was seeing her, all I could say was that it was just a matter of a few hours, and I didn't want to ruin them.

"I promise…" I said and walked out.

Dad opened an expensive bottle of scotch; he was not someone you expect to be even an occasional drinker. I quietly sat opposite him on another sofa.

"Soda or water?" He asked.

I needed nothing. I could consume it without diluting. After all, that's what I'd been doing for the past seven months. But I didn't want him to get hurt, at least not at that moment.

"Soda dad!"

He poured about fifty ml large scotch and another fifty ml of soda for himself and for me. He knew how much we needed to pass through the bloody promise which I considered senseless.

After consuming three consecutive drinks without uttering a word, I finally managed to pull out the question I wanted to ask.

"Dad! Do you know why she did this?"

"Yes, Dhruv! But I'm not allowed to tell you."

M and her bloody promises, I hate you M!

"Will it do something good?"

"May be later, yes!"

"Okay…"

And then three straight shots! My eyes were tipsy and so were his. Mom was already in bed, weeping secretly as she did all the time.

The bottle was empty. I finished my first and last drink with her dad, someone whom I was supposed to look after. She unwillingly freed me from my responsibility and I still don't know why. I just hope she had a bloody good reason for doing that.

I stood up to leave, but not before helping him reach his bed.

"I love you, son, always remember that." He quivered and said while I put him in his bed.

"I love you too, dad!"

And I walked out in tears, the moment I'll hate for the rest of my life.

The festival is over; Ansh and Angie are married and now probably on the way to their honeymoon. Angie somehow didn't give me the exact information on their departure date and time and although I wanted to see them off to their flight, Dhruv refused and that made me angry. I knew he didn't want me to spoil my work. He cares about me. He genuinely does.

But then, why did he ask me to take a day off? What was it for which he wanted me for an *entire day?* I don't know yet, but I've to figure it out. Is this the day? When I will hear the big call from him? No, I don't think so. I don't think he can. Not until he is finished working on the atrocious part. I know it is taking him longer than usual, but I certainly empathise with his agony – because somewhere inside, I'm having the same. Even I'm unsure of how I'd be able to read it at once or if I'd be able to read it at all. I don't know. Just like I don't know where he'll take me. Will we be alone? I hope so – but we have never been alone for an *entire day!*

He drives near, moves his car closer to me. I sit inside and close the door. I look at him…

Jeez…His eyes…they are red…blood red…swollen and blood red!

Oh my! He has done it. He has finished it. He has been crying all night, but he has done it. I – along with Ansh and Angie – was skeptical about how he'd do it; but he has, he has finished what he promised.

139

So that's why he asked me to take a day off? May be, but I need to ask him where we're going because the route we've taken does not lead us to Cafe Piano.

"Where are we going, Dhruv?" I softly ask.

"My place, at Baroda."

What!! My heart jumps at my throat. Why is he taking me there? Just the two of us? I don't know what to make out of this. And before I say something, he clears my mind.

"Don't worry Nilu! It's not what you are thinking, and we'll be back in a few hours. Trust me."

I know; not trusting him would be the last thing on my mind, but all my thoughts are running. Is this what I'm thinking? Is this the big day? I'll have to wait for probably two hours to find out. But I'm happy; I always wanted to see his home there. I want to see the room where Ansh and Angie ascertained each other completely, and the sofa Dhruv mentioned, where he and M watched *P.S. I Love You* in each other's arms. I want to see the table where he proposed to M, which she mentioned even in our last meeting. I'm both exhilarated and nervous at the same time; what if he proposes me there? In the same house and under the same roof? That would be more than anything he could ever give me. All the struggle and pain that we are going through, there would be no better end to this. I want that – desperately.

In between the whirlwind of thoughts in my mind, he hands his iPhone to me.

"Read the final part."

"What? Here? I mean in the car?" I say appraising my nervousness.

"Yes, Nilu, we've almost one-and-a-half hour to reach there. Let's use it."

And I start reading.

12 February:
The goodbye kiss

It was a quiet and peaceful morning. The clock was ticking and it was the only sound I could hear. I wasn't feeling her breaths. I already sensed it. I woke up and looked at her. She was gone. I moved my hand close to her eyes, but *Wait!* She moved her head a bit. I felt blessed with a new life. She was not gone. I had one more day. She finally opened her eyes and smiled at me.

"Mithu?" She was barely able to speak now and almost mumbled.

"Yes, baby. I'm right here."

"The time has come," she said and tears rolled down her eyes. I wiped her tears, but failed to sense the amount of tears I kept shedding, which I did not want to wipe. I wanted to cry. Only they could help me with the pain of losing her.

"Mithu?"

"Hmm." A blunt sound came out as my voice chocked within my throat.

"It's the time for a goodbye kiss."

I know my love! But how can I see you going?

"Are you in hurry, M? Or can you wait for five minutes?"

"I could wait all my life for you Mithu, if it was in my hand. But I don't think our God is so cruel that he will not give me five more minutes."

Our God, the concept of our God was simple. We both believed in one God, who is beyond religions, mosques, temples, and churches. Our God lives within ourselves and within every other being. And yes, he was not so cruel after all. He gave us more than five minutes.

I'll always be grateful to him that he gave us the chance of saying goodbye. This way, he proved his existence to me. Otherwise, she'd died five days ago. But he gave me all those moments to live my life with – along with those bloody promises. But you have to pay your price and perhaps those promises were my price.

"Mithu!"

"Hmm?"

"Say something Mithu! I do not have much time left."

I grabbed her hand and kissed it.

"You are still not done with kisses, right?"

"No, never!"

"So… How was it Mithu?"

"How was what?"

"The entire quest of us?"

"You know how it was baby. You know, I could do anything possible to change our fate because somehow I feel that I couldn't give you everything I wanted to. Love, passion, intimacy…I feel there are so many things I've missed and failed in giving you."

"Hey Mithu, shhh! Please don't say that. You have given me more than I could possibly ever desire. I know we are not having a perfect end of our story, but I assure you that I will be around. I'm not done with you yet. You'll feel me around someday. Now tell me, how was I? Praise me, compliment me…because I want to relive those moments for one last time." She winked with a smile. *Girls! They want compliments even on the deathbed…*

But what I said was much more than compliments and praises. I made her relive our whole journey – of course with tears in our eyes. I had tears of all my life in those last twelve days but as I said, I did not mind crying.

"Our journey… It started with your tears, remember? (her face frowned, snaps at me). You were crying in the middle of that road, when I saw you from my car, I thought *How dumb is She?* (she gets more angry, gasping in fury). But then I realised that she was not crying for herself. She was crying for the stress it could cause her father. Though it was still hard to understand that for an irresponsible and insensitive guy like me, I somehow found it cute (she blushes) and then all that night, we were chasing each other's eyes (she smiles, yeah, we did). Although at first, I thought it may be infatuation because I did not believe in love at first sight. But I knew this wasn't just any other attraction; it was something more than that (she blushes even more). You know you were not the first girl in my life and because of those bloody promises, not the last (she now grins, flaunting pride for that bloody promise). But, you were special. Because I still get butterflies in my stomach when I look into your eyes. I still get as fascinated as I was when I saw you for the first time. I felt it was my duty to never let that smile drop from your face. I always wanted to make you laugh. Every minute, I was thinking about how to impress you and when I saw my plans working, I would literally jump with joy (her eyes moistened, but she hadn't dropped her smile. She still gets impressed by me). Then a big day came, I proposed to you. First through a text message and then at my home, by looking into your eyes, just the way you wanted (her nose and cheeks are getting red. She is blushing more than ever). On that day, I kissed you for the first time. It was like a never-ending ecstatic excursion. I still can feel those lips. Pink, wide and gorgeous. Oh shit I'm getting butterflies, even now (She tightened her grip on my hand, as if she would never want to leave them). Then it became regular. Kisses, fights and a competition. Who's smarter? And I won it by outsmarting you most of the times (She now gets angry; twitches her face, clenches her teeth and smiles too. A combination good enough to instigate me to smooch her which I did... and continued). Ansh, Angie, you and I – the fantastic four. No amount of money can buy the time we shared together. We were extremely romantic and crazy enough to blow each other's minds and passionate enough to kiss each other in front of them. I think they were more shameless, what say? (She widens her smile, nods her head in affirmation). It was going like a desired dream when the time came…you left me. I should've tried to understand you and should've known you well enough that you could never leave me like this. I should've remained calm and sought the reason. But I turned into a jerk. After seven forgettable months with alcohol, drugs and dopes, our God was kind enough to give me that wake-up call through that accident at the right time (heavy tears started dropping from her eyes). Sorry baby, for hurting you, but it was also a part of my love for you. No matter how drunk I got, no matter how many cigarettes I smoked, no matter how many drugs I took, I always failed in erasing your memories. Not a single day passed when I did not feel for you; your sharp blue almond eyes, your delicate red nose and ears, your silky golden hair, your everlasting and enchanting smile. I just couldn't get rid of you. Even though I tried to hate you a lot, but I could never really succeed in that. My love, you were a part of me. How could I cut you off (she is still in heavy tears and not even trying to restrain it)? When I came back, you did not have much time left and I did not have enough time left with you. The last two weeks, my love, I can proudly say that you've changed me and my life in those two weeks. When I first saw you like this, I was a person in unbearable grief and turmoil. In these past few days, you've taught me what life really is; through this story which I wrote for you and through our new family that will be strangers again from now and that's because of you (this time I snapped at her, she lowered her wet eyes). I feel like I'm born again as a better person than I used to be. I grew up. I can feel that I'm more mature and calm than I used to be. Still, a part of me will always hate one word because of you – sacrifice. I'll always hate that word and a part of me will always hate you for choosing death over me (she is now weeping - in extreme disappointment. I realised I should have slurred my words). My love! But you gave me a new birth. The wisdom I got in these last fifteen days, will always be with me like shadow as well as a gift from you. Thank you, my love! Thank you, for coming into my life and making it wonderful (she is now smiling. Gripping my hand as tightly as she can and trying hard to move her head to kiss my hand. I gave it to her and she kissed my hand and her tears moistened my hand)."

"Now kiss me for the last time…." She softly demanded after having a long session of kissing my hand.

I took her in my arms and kissed her. It was the most passionate, ecstatic and breathtaking kiss we ever shared. It was everlasting and I just kept going, till her tongue stopped moving inside my mouth. She was gone. I knew it, but I still kept going. She had left her body, her lips were not moving at all but I still wasn't stopping. After several minutes when I started having problem in breathing, I parted my lips from hers. I kissed her head for the last time. I slowly put her down; her eyes were already closed. She was gone. I lost my girlfriend in between our heavenly kiss. I hope it stays with her – and stays with me too.

I packed my stuff quickly and opened the door.

Dad was waiting for me outside. He understood everything as he saw me and hugged me tightly. We both fell on each other's shoulders in our cries. A wind of agony rose inside our hearts, and we both were literally growling in pain. Mom came there and understanding what would have happened, went inside. I could hear her cry of pain. The pain of losing the only child cannot be understood by anyone else other than the parents. I saw it. From the past twelve days, I had been an intact part of this family.

And she took them away from me with her bloody promises.

"Can we have our last breakfast together? Can you make those omelettes for the last time?" Dad asked. Surprisingly, he was in no hurry for the cremation of his only daughter. She could wait to turn into ashes for a while, but that was our last time. I knew it, they knew it. To be honest, I hated that bloody promise more than anything at that time. Her cremation process, I don't know when and how it happened because I was not there. I wanted to but I knew that was her father's legal and virtuous right. Once again, she was just a stranger to me. I had nothing of her other than our memories.

"Of course, dad!" I went in the kitchen and made those omelettes for us. We sat together, and ate it, quietly. I realised it was saltier today. I wanted to apologise, but I didn't need to. They knew very well from where that salt taste was coming. I think at that time, we all were running out of words. He finished a little earlier, went inside and brought an envelope for me.

"This is something for you," He said and handed me the envelope. It was a letter from her. I started reading.

Dear Dhruv,

You are reading this letter, which means I'm far away, yet so close. There are some things that I never felt like telling you, but now I think I should. In this short journey of my life, I'm feeling proud and pleasured to think about those substantial moments with you. Every moment that I shared with you, with our friends, were blissful and went like a dream for me. I lived my life with dignity, joy and without having a single regret and I want you to live the same. I might have taken those promises from you... Well, I know you'll keep it well enough. My intention of writing this was to inform you that when you leave this house, I want you to take nothing of me except my memories. Not even this letter. Give it to my father. Have a great and wonderful life Mithu! See you in your memories. Bye.

My tears had made that letter almost wet. I handed it to her father whom I could not call dad anymore. I pulled out my diary and gave it to him. "This is all I have, except her memories. This is the story I wrote for her, and I know I'll be able to do that again. But I want you to have this, I want you to read our love story before the entire world does and that's all I can give you, sir!" I saw how that last word "sir" pained him.

"I'll be waiting for your name in one of those books son!" he said shedding uncontrollable tears.

"How do you know about that?"

"She was planning it for the past four months. She used to tell me so much about your art of storytelling," he said amidst sobs.

"She was the only one who believed in that."

He nodded positively; still the three of us were in tears. I felt that I couldn't take it anymore.

"I think I need to go now, sir!" I said and picked my bags.

"All the best, son!" they both said. I touched their feet, took their blessings and left them once and for all.

I keep weeping, thinking about how hard it could be for Dhruv and her parents to see her go. I somehow feel nice about not being there when she left us – but that didn't keep me from missing her and secretly crying for her.

Dhruv holds my hand and tightens his grip. I gaze at him and realise he's in tears too!

"It's okay Nilu! It's over now!" He mumbles. I know he's lying, it's not over and I certainly don't want this to be over. He doesn't know the fact that I loved M – if not more than him – as much as him. But I stay quiet, not because I want to hide the truth from him and you all. I'm dying to tell him the only secret I ever kept from him. I just can't…maybe someday, may be…

I realise we are about to reach his home and my heart starts thumping as we move closer. He's now smiling; thank god! But now that I've read the final part, why is he taking me there? Is this what I think? Is this the big day? Perhaps this is. I don't know any other reason for him to drive me here.

I'm having goosebumps. If I'm going to relive the moments I imagined being M in his narration, I promise to be dancing naked in my shower the next day – no, not with him, not this soon.

But I'm nervous as hell. Is he going to kiss me there? Right after proposing to me! He's definitely not! He and M had a year of being an unauthorised couple before they kissed and he knows it very well. But what if he does? What if he kisses me there? Goosebumps aren't stopping…Jeez, I hope he doesn't hear my heartbeats; they are so loud and I'm unable to control them.

I see Ansh and Angie's car as we reach. What? I thought they went on their honeymoon! What the hell are they doing here? And if they are here, that means no kissing. (Why do I feel sad?)

"Ansh and Angie?" I mumble and he nods.

"I thought they were on their honeymoon!"

He smiles.

"They are…"

"What? Here?"

They come out to greet us as they hear us. Angie in her nightwear and Ansh in shorts. Seems like they just woke up. Dhruv is right, they seem like they are on their honeymoon. But why here? What about Singapore?

"Hey sweetie!"Angie greets me as she comes out.

"What's going on Angie? You guys were supposed to be in Singapore!"

She smirked.

"We are leaving tomorrow dear! And I deserve some respect. I spent the next night after my reception preparing things because your big guy wanted it large."

"What preparation???"

"You'll have to come inside to see that Nilu!"Ansh said from behind.

After parking his car, Dhruv joins me as we go inside.

Oh my goodness! The entire floor is illuminated (decorated, illuminated is used for lights) with rose petals and the walls are decorated with our childhood pictures with heart shaped balloons around them. I thought he'd do it the same way, but he didn't take me to his dining room. Instead, they took me to the first floor into a dark room.

As we reached, Angie turned on a few switches and I saw my childhood picture on the screen! It's his home theatre! This is so romantic!

Ansh increases the volume and I hear a soft evolving piano music. When did he plan this? I thought he'd been shattered and distressed after writing the final part.

I see a line emerging from the centre: *You were this, when the last time I didn't know you.*

Oh yeah, he was right! I was three or four years then.

Then I see a picture of us together in school. He had it! I thought he'd have dumped it. I have the same picture with a heart shape cut in my secret diary. That's fascinating and I flush when I glance at him. He indicates me to look back at the screen. Huh, the control freak Dhruv…but my Dhruv.

Our image gets blurred on the celluloid and with the music involved being more instrumental, I see the words flashing,

We never needed a reason to laugh, to make each other smile and to love each other,

We loved each other even when we didn't know what love was,

But we knew, that all we needed to do when life got tough, was to hold each other's hand…

Then I see a picture of me lifted in his arms, it was of the 'Sangeet night' of Ansh and Angie.

The line flashes afterwards, which makes me quiver with goosebumps.

I was shattered with agony, disparity and agitation and that's when you returned,

One step away from going crazy, but something held me there,

I looked back and learned it was your hand; it was you, who covered me in your secure arms without being asked,

Something you're doing since we were twelve,

Now can I have the privilege of doing the same with you for the rest of my life?

The music stops, lights go on, I stand pale, with wet eyes.

All three of them are staring at me, waiting for me to answer. I don't know how the hell it came out, when I said,

"That's it?"

Angie guffaws and Dhruv is standing with his mouth wide open, astonished.

"I told you Dhruv, it's not enough. You guys always undermine girls like us."

Dhruv is clueless, looking at me with disappointment.

Okay now, I've to tell him the truth, I cannot see him like this.

"Sorry Dhruv, it was at Angie's behest, I had to say this. While we were stepping up, she asked me to say it."

Dhruv took a sigh of relief. Oh my, don't baby!

"By the way, yes…"I add.

"Oh Nilu, why did you say it? I was planning to cash more fun with it,"Angie pouts.

"That was not funny Angie!" He snaps at her.

"Of course it was. Look at you Dhruv, you've lost all your humour. You were never like this!"She grimaces.

I hold her hand to stop; she apparently doesn't know that he has written it. I tell Dhruv to hand me his phone and I give it to her to read.

Meanwhile, Dhruv and I come to the kitchen, preparing our lunch while Ansh and Angie are sitting in the dining room. After preparing Ansh and Angie's favourite paneer sabji, I go to the dining room and find Angie's head on Ansh's shoulders, as they both are crying. I go and rub her back. She holds my hand tightly and I too crumble in tears.

When Dhruv comes with rotis and sees us like this, he doesn't say anything. He just places everything on the table and sits. In a while I too join him.

A cheerful celebration has turned into a sorrowful mourning, which we don't mind – it is for M – and we know what she means to all of us. Dhruv holds my hand and smiles, surprisingly. He looks calmer than the three of us.

"Calm down guys, this is not how she would've wanted a day like this to be. You were right Angie, I had lost all my fun and while you three were…mmm…crying here, I thought about something. Why did she make me promise those things, I don't know yet why but I have an idea now! May be because she thought if I go to her parents every weekend or so, I would no longer be able to move on. I'd make peace with my sorrows and would never be able to move further. She wanted me – and having said that she clearly meant us – to be happy. She didn't want us to make peace with our sorrows and to get accustomed to them. She wanted us to move on; she wanted us to imagine her smiling face when we think of her, not her dying face. She was a great girlfriend and more than that, a great human being. So now, let's take a vow, that we'll remember only our happy memories with her and will try our best not to cry for the loss. Let's promise each other that."

I glanced at Ansh and Angie, they were still in tears. Perhaps they were the last; perhaps this promise will work, but before we take this promise, I've to tell him the truth. He's in a mood of acceptance now and I can't commence our relationship based on a foundation of lies. Today's the day, he accepted his feelings for me, so let today be the day they all learn the truth and let fate decide our future.

"I've something to say Dhruv! But after you narrate the final two chapters about Ansh and Angie. How they got their perfect ending."

"Okay." He says, a little surprised and after we finish our lunch, he starts reading.

Angie is literally jumping on the couch, hastily as she can't wait to hear how Dhruv penned her dream ending in his words.

On the twelfth day, Dhruv went home, with a miserably destroyed heart and with eyes swollen red. The arrival of his car made his entire family to come out. When he stepped out, and his parents saw him like that – especially his eyes – they knew that something had gone terribly wrong with him. They all wanted to ask, but couldn't!

They could by all means empathise with his agony and knew how broken he was from inside. They just embraced him as he was and led him to his room. His father was furious and compassionate at the same time; furious for allowing misery to take him over and let disparity take roots in his core. Dhruv could see the disdain for him in his father's eyes, but he didn't blame him by any mean.

After all, he hasn't lost his wife...

It was afternoon, which turned into a calm night in no time. Dhruv just sat in his dark room and wept. His mom first came to console him. She thought it was because of the detention, which he got due to low attendance or perhaps for being absent in the final exams. She told him that it's all going to be okay. However, like everyone else, she didn't know why he missed his exams and unlike her husband, older son and his wife, she didn't want to know the reason. Being a mother, she thought everything her son did was due to some reason and even thinking about seeking those reasons from him could be the contempt of motherly love.

Dhruv's brother, like his father, was angry with him. Being a radiologist himself, he well understood the damage caused by repetition of an entire year – that too by not appearing in the exams. He, like his father, was in no mood of seeing his brother, and Dhruv didn't blame him for that too.

He too, like his father, hadn't lost his wife.

But Dhruv felt sorry for letting him down. He promised to be back, being a better and stronger person and all he did that day was to weep for his lost love.

Dhruv's sister-in-law was worried for him the most. She had known him for seven long years and he was never like this. Sometimes irritating her with his humour, but he had always been a caring and cheerful soul. Her affection for Dhruv was motherly as well as of a friend, and a friend inside her knew that he had been through the worst possible things than he could ever imagine. She knew that from being an immature and irresponsible macho boy to a fat weeping machine, he has lost something; something, which was most valuable to him and more than that, he has lost himself with it! She too, like her husband, couldn't concentrate on her work and both returned early from their hospital. They both were worried that if he continued to be like this, he'd soon reach the final stage of depression. They had to do something; something to cheer him up.

And they had to do it soon.

The next day was no different. He kept weeping inside his dark room; his mother too kept weeping for his son, his father and brother kept getting angrier and were disappointed, and his sister-in-law kept getting worried.

Dhruv's brother, Dr. Brijesh was driving his car home with his wife, Dr. Hetanshi, who was sitting beside him.

"You talked to him? Got to know what the matter is?" Dr. Brijesh asked. He had been angry earlier, but at that moment, he started getting worried for his little brother.

"No, he doesn't speak to anyone, not even mom!" Dr. Hetanshi replied with concern in her voice.

"At first, after his accident, I thought this was another one of his dramas but then he eloped for twelve days and came back like this. I think something terrible has happened to him, could it be his girlfriend?"

"He doesn't discuss his love life with me or anyone, but he mentioned to me once that he broke up with her seven months ago. I don't think this can be about her, unless that girl is married to some other guy now."

"Hmm, and he cannot take that defeat, that I know for sure. But I don't think he'd go to this extent only because of jealousy."

"May be we should take him out tomorrow and try to talk to him about this!"

"Good idea, but before that, I'll have to screw him for ruining my Valentine's Day!" He chuckled, taking a glance at his wife who replied with a brief smile, but concern for Dhruv was still clouded on her face.

I'm surely going to screw him now!

That Valentine's Day, Dr. Brijesh and Dr. Hetanshi had no desire to spend it with Dhruv, but they did. They wanted to show him how happy the world is; they wanted him to be happy like everyone else; they wanted to show him that break-ups happen, we get hurt by the people we love, but even with all those wretchedness and hardships, we must continue to pursue our destiny, our dreams. They were right, Dhruv thought; however, he also knew that they were oblivious of certain things. Destiny…he had found his destiny when he found M two years back and the only dream he was able to achieve was M.

He'd lost his destiny and dream, he had lost his love. But that outing helped him a lot, probably more than he imagined.

He was sitting on the backseat – as his brother decided to keep him away from the wheels for some time due to that accident – his eyes glittered on seeing some college folks who were wearing same colour T-shirts. That reminded him of the fantastic four. How he, Ansh, Angie and M used to make everyone around them anxious of their friendship and of course Harsh, Shilpan and Aakash, without whom this entire journey was distant.

In the afternoon, they watched a romantic movie. Dhruv caught several couples kissing in the theatre; that too reminded her of M. No, not because she liked being kissed in the theatre; in fact, she hated it. Once when Dhruv tried to take advantage of her in the theatre, she slapped her own boyfriend – leaving him embarrassed and agitated for a week. She later explained that why she thought kissing in theatre was cowardly. She liked being kissed at various places, but never in a theatre. Dhruv touched his cheek where he had gotten that slap and smiled like it had happened a minute ago.

After finishing the movie, while walking out, he saw many lovers walking holding their hands. That's something she loved the most; holding Dhruv's hand was something she could do for an entire day, especially on days like Valentine's Day – where girls go out in sexier clothes and quoting "men will be men". She and Angie had faced a lot of trouble to keep their boys under their nails.

Then he saw many boys giving their girls flowers and chocolates; that reminded him of those ten days of chocolate fight. That was the cutest fight he remembered out of all others. Her favourite orchids that reminded him of the way she used to smell them every morning on her deathbed. He from the very beginning knew that it was about her faith; her faith of being able to smell Dhruv's aroma in those odourless beauty corps. She knew how cute he found her doing it and she knew how long the kiss she was going to get afterwards.

It was all-perfect then.

After having an entire day without a single conversation with Dhruv, his brother and sister-in-law finally gathered the courage to ask what they wanted to over dinner.

"Dhruv!" Dr. Hetanshi gently spoke, keeping her voice low but clear.

"Yes, Bhabhi?"

"How's your girlfriend?"

He thought about it. How would she be right now? Where could she possibly be? And he realised there were few questions on earth, which were still unanswered. But he knew why she had asked that and he knew it by the way she and his brother were looking at him, trying to breach his eyes, searching for the right answer.

But they were too inexperienced in knowing how it feels to lose someone you love.

"She must be fine, wherever she is." That's all he could say keeping a smile on his face.

That's all they spoke that day. They were ensured now that it was a break up and his brother was now angrier at him for jeopardising his entire life due to an immature practice called break up.

But Dhruv didn't blame them. He had been in their shoes – of blaming someone he loved for seven months without knowing the truth. He knew how much they cared for him and how much he meant to them.

Although something went different after that question; something irked inside of him. Did he see her today? Yes, he did. In those college buddies, he saw her; in those fighting couples, he saw her; in those girls who were taking flowers and chocolates, he saw her; in every girl who was holding her lover's hands, he saw her; even in those couples who were kissing each other in the theatre, he felt that slap. He saw M everywhere today; because there was one thing common between all of them and him – Love!

In every single event where affection was felt, he saw her. He was not alone; there were countless Ms and Dhruvs he saw that day. He realised that as long as he succeeds in doing justice to their story, which he had promised, he could keep her alive. She was not dead, not yet, it was now up to him, he could make her live in people's mind forever or he could kill her by breaking his promise – which he didn't even consider.

The challenge was hard – being a below average medical student – it was nearly impossible for him to go in the territory of the people who were far more talented and experienced than him. He decided to work hard and read several books, first to see what he was missing and how their work and writing was different and better than his.

But before that, he had an engagement to spoil. Yes, Angie's engagement which was scheduled within a few days. He knew how he could stop her and was determined to do the same.

A few days passed and Dhruv's family was pleased by the way he had improved. He was no longer a crybaby – at least not when they were watching him. He had started working out, reading his study books and a few novels as well. He had been a voracious reader and they were happy – like never before – to see him as he was.

He wore his tux, put on a black satin tie and made the final adjustments. He had to look handsome and aristocratic; after all, he had an engagement to ruin.

He looked at himself in the mirror and said,

'See M, your Mithu is going to keep his promise. I'm sure you're somewhere around watching this.'

He checked his phone and there was a message from Nilu.

"Try to go easy there!" Dhruv smiled – knowing the concern behind this message.

He almost forgot her and didn't even know that he had the charm in him to even interact with girls anymore. A couple of failed attempts gave a life to his dilemma; but then he had a friend request from a familiar name. At first he could not believe himself, but when he clicked on the picture, to his surprise, it was her – Nirali Shah, his first crush, first female friend, first love, almost first everything. Had it been any other girl, he'd have ended up with a tagline of either bore or too formal – but as he knew it well – things with her had always been different. She was just the same as he had left her in school – same warmth, care and fondness in her eyes and words. The best part was that she was still single.

Why?

When she first heard about his relationship with M and her demise, she was in tears, but she wasn't surprised – as she already knew that something wrong was happening with Dhruv. He was obliged to accept that, she too – by holding his hand just like the old days – played a big part in his recuperation.

He stepped down and saw his family members waiting for him to join them for breakfast. His father flaunted a proud smile when he saw Dhruv in tux as – he believed – it was an indication of him becoming a man from a boy. His brother, however, was not completely convinced with him, but he too appreciated the efforts he was putting in. His sister-in-law was happy – if not exhilarated – with the change she was seeing in him; his mother, for her having him around was everything and she was now leaving no stone unturned to fill in her lapses – as she thought she had failed as a mother.

"So, everything set?"His father asked. It was his set up. He didn't admit to Dhruv that he had influenced many people to get Mr. Shah a reputed job, but Dhruv knew he did.

"Thanks dad! If I succeed in what I aim to, it will all be because of you," Dhruv coyly answered.

"I talked with his company; they said they were really impressed by his presentation. Besides, I don't want your gratitude. I want your commitment. Promise me that you will focus on your studies from now on."

Promises and more promises!

"I will dad! But before that I've got to finish things; what you have spent on me will not be wasted dad. That's all I can promise right now. I'll clear the MBBS. Now if you all excuse me, I have an engagement to spoil." He chortled and stood up, took his car keys and started walking towards the door.

"Dhruv!" His brother called,

"Yes, Bhai?" Dhruv turned around.

"Welcome back." He said, and Dhruv nodded with a smile and walked out.

As per the plan, Shilpan, Aakash and Harsh were ready and were waiting for him outside his house. He was seeing them after eight months. Dhruv had fought with them and he knew he owed an apology to each of them. As soon as he went near, he realised that they had failed to bring Ansh. He was still in no-talking mode with him and especially with Angie.

"Hello seniors, wanna take my intro first?" He smirked, knowing that they all had passed the final year exams while he was detained for one year.

"Shut up Gajju! By the way Ansh…" Shilpan said, and Dhruv interrupted,

"Didn't come, I know, this male ego, I tell you."

"And look who's talking!" Aakash quipped, fluttering his sarcastic brows at Dhruv. Dhruv embraced the allegations with a short bow.

"He even sent his greetings for Angie instead, can you believe that?" Harsh sighed in consternation.

"Yes, he can!" This time it was from Shilpan, you can't be best friends without constantly insulting each other.

"I guess he is overreacting…" Aakash offered.

"He's not; it's just another one of his dramas. He loves Angie more than anything else, but he also knows that he has us to do his job," Dhruv replied.

"Exactly, so let's move and get this girl for that bastard!" Harsh suggested with a wide grin.

"Yup, but before that, you guys deserve an apology from me. For all those shitty things I'd done over the past few months to you and to everyone else," Dhruv meekly said. None of them seemed moved. Instead, they laughed.

"You're not the good guy Gajju, you've always been a fucker and will remain the same, no matter how hard you try, so don't bother yourself." Aakash sneered.

"How many times will I have to apologise for your one night stand with those ropes?" Dhruv retorted with a wink, leaving Aakash grunting in fury.

"Oops, hard memories!" Shilpan binged in.

In a moment Aakash, Shilpan and Harsh stepped into Shilpan's car and Dhruv in his own. Dhruv couldn't help himself but smile at what was coming; he knew – as he had planned – that this was going to be fun.

He drove to Angie's home where Mr. and Mrs. Shah – Angie's parents had already packed their bags and were waiting for the boys to come.

Mr. Shah's elder brother, Angie's Badepapa had already asked him to leave their house and the company first, if he wanted her to marry Ansh. He knew this was not going to be easy – almost impossible – unless Dhruv's father didn't dial a few numbers and made the process quick. Being an IITian, he always had the job opportunities, but he gave his twenty-five years to his family business and everyone in the office knew that it was him, who brought their company up with his marketing skills and intellectual decisions. Everyone except his brother knew it, and knew that he could go to any extent to save his daughter's life; his only daughter, his priceless and immense source of happiness was sacrificing her own life for him and he couldn't allow it.

After stepping out, the first thing Dhruv did was to congratulate Mr. Shah for his new home where he was about to take them – but not before kidnapping Angie from her engagement. Yes, that was the plan. He was probably the first father in the world to kidnap his own daughter from her engagement and that too, for her boyfriend.

After loading their bags into Dhruv and Shilpan's car boots, they all were ready for a big hijack – of which Angie was completely oblivious. Mr. and Mrs. Shah sat in Dhruv's car and they started heading towards the banquet hall.

Dhruv's hands were calmly moving on the steering wheel and he was providing a smooth, quiet and blissful ride.

"Dhruv, how are you now?" Mr. Shah broke the ice. Dhruv knew what he was talking about and he knew that this would be coming – perhaps not that soon!

He remained silent, waiting for them to be more specific.

"This must be hard for you, son! Coming here and…" Mrs. Shah added.

"It was a job I had to do auntie. I could do anything to get Angie out of there and Mr. Shah, I mean it, anything!" He snapped. Mr. Shah understood what he meant. Rishi, Angie's only cousin could be troublesome and Dhruv was determined to be a trouble-shooter, regardless of any consequences.

"You've my word son, I won't intervene." This was the reply Dhruv was hoping for. He smiled at him and after a brief moment of silence, Mrs. Shah tried to bring that up again; this time, being specific.

"She was a great girl son, I'm sure she would be happy to see you like this again." They waited for Dhruv's reaction before they exhaled and were relieved to see him smile, not in tears.

"She undoubtedly was, auntie! Apart from Ansh and Angie, I'm doing this for her too!"

They reached the banquet and saw a welcoming banner, which read,

Betrothal ceremony of
Angel Shah
&
Vishal Shah

Dhruv gazed at it and asked, "Why Mr. Shah? Why Vishal?"

"It was more like a business deal, Dhruv. His father is politically the most powerful person of our community and my brother knows how to earn brownie points from this.

"We'll have to make sure that they don't hurt you after this." Dhruv was concerned; he tilted his head to one side to check if his friends were behind him or not.

Shilpan, Aakash and Harsh entered after Dhruv and Angie's parents. They rushed in like a force. Rishi – Angie's cousin – saw them and raced towards them.

"What the hell are you doing here?" He arched his fumed brows at Dhruv, but Mr. Shah interrupted.

"He's with us."

"He's not invited here."

"Son, I think it's my daughter's engagement, so let me decide whom to invite."

Rishi reiterated; Dhruv smirked at him and headed towards the stage.

Angie looked down in shame as he saw them, having no courage to look into any of their eyes.

"Hey Vishal, I want you to meet Dhruv!" Mr. Shah introduced.

"How can I forget him? Because of him and his brother, I had to spend six months in jail," he scoffed, putting a sarcastic smile on Dhruv's face.

"I hope you learned how to drive after that," Dhruv leered at him.

"Eat your food and go to hell," Vishal grumbled.

"He's leaving now, actually. We all are leaving. We are here to take our daughter, that's all. After that, you can enjoy your food," Mr. Shah said and grabbed Angie's hand. Before she could understand anything, they started walking.

"Hey, hey, hey, what the hell is going on?" Rishi who was observing everything from a yard away, tried to take charge on his own uncle. But before he could reach Mr. Shah, Dhruv obstructed him underway and charged a punch to his face, leaving his nose bleeding.

"Now you know what I can do with my tiny muscles, consider yourself lucky that I'm not in my best shape. Let's go Mr. Shah!" He groaned.

"Just a minute, Dhruv!" Mr. Shah said and walked towards his father.

"You had just one son who cared about you, dad. Today you lost him. And Motabhai, I'll not allow you or anyone else to ruin my daughter's life. You asked me to leave the house, I already did and now don't even dare to look at my daughter!" He admonished, grabbed Angie's hand again and turned to Rishi before walking out.

"Rishi, your mother never wanted you to be as ruthless and heartless like your father; but your lust for power eventually brought you down to his level. Your mother didn't commit suicide because of the guilt of cheating your father; it's a lie that you were told all your life. You are an embarrassment she hated in her husband."

Dhruv was driving, Mr. Shah was sitting beside him and Angie was crying on her mother's shoulder on the backseat, oblivious of where they were heading.

When they reached Mr. Shah's new house, which was allotted by his company, Angie was completely dumbstruck by what was going around. They stepped out and Mr. Shah shook his hand with the manager – along with a few other families – who were sent to hand him the keys of the house and the company car.

"Mr. Prasoon, I along with all our staff welcome you in our neighbourhood. Here are your house and car keys," the Manager said while handing him the keys.

Angie, who was standing alongside Dhruv and his friends, went pale with her jaw wide open. Mr. Shah went to her and handed her the keys with a big ear-to-ear grin on his face.

"Seems like we succeeded in surprising my princess, right Dhruv?" She gazed at Dhruv as Mr. Shah quipped.

"Fair point! Well made, Mr. Shah," Dhruv nodded his head with affirmation.

Angie broke into tears and hugged Dhruv and his friends as soon as she learned what they had done for her.

She then turned to Dhruv, "You know Dhruv, today I was missing her more than ever. As I was thinking about her, you guys entered." She said and hugged his best friend, Dhruv, who was also missing M.

Hope you're somewhere around, M!

She then turned to Shilpan, Harsh and Aakash, "Thanks for everything guys,"

"Ah, that's nothing. We could have never let you marry that bastard, you know that. By the way Angie, Ansh…" Shilpan stopped in between; he was unable to finish his line.

"I know, refused to come and he doesn't want to see my face; I know that too." She shook her head and wiped her tears. Mr. Shah heard her and put his hand on her head.

"Everything will be fine princess! Now boys, if you could help us with the luggage." Mr. Shah relentlessly moved her attention.

After setting everything by evening and demobilising herself from the jewellery and traditional *choli*, Angie and her mom were placing their dishes on the table for dinner. There had been only a few occasions, out in restaurants where they had dinner together – never at home.

Angie was amused, sitting in her new house, considerably smaller than her old home but large enough to let them breathe freely.

"So princess, happy now?" Mr. Shah broke the ice.

"I'm running out of words to thank you dad!" She replied as firmly as she could.

"So why is our princess still sad?" Her mother was the first one to notice,

"Don't tell me you wanted to marry Vishal," Mr. Shah quipped, trying to move her thoughts from the disparity.

"Jeez...papa! I'm just thinking about..."

"Ansh, we know that."

"Hmm."

"He'll come back, just give him some time."

"I hope so papa!"

"Don't tell me you're going to die single if he doesn't come back."

Without any reservation, she replied, "You know papa, I will!"

After dinner, Mr. Shah was sitting cross-legged, watching news when someone knocked the door. He stood up but Angie was swift in reaching the door. She was feared and dumbstruck by whom she saw there – Rishi. Had he come to hurt them? No, she couldn't let him do it. She stood firmly obstructing his way in.

"What are you doing here?" She snapped at him and to her surprise, he didn't revert. Instead, he looked down and remained silent.

Mr. Shah came from behind and said, "Cool down Angie, I called him here."

Surprised, Angie went aside, making way for him. He came inside, sat on the sofa and asked for a glass of water. After consuming two glasses of water, he looked at Mr. Shah and asked what he came for, "You said you had something related to my mother?"

Mr. Shah nodded, called out to his wife, and asked her to bring that letter. Neither Angie nor Rishi knew a thing about it. Whenever Angie asked her mother about what happened to Rishi's mother, she changed the topic. All she had coaxed out in twenty-three years was that something terrible, really terrible happened to her, and Rishi was told – obviously by his father that her mother cheated on his father and committed suicide in guilt. But somewhere in his heart, he knew that his mother wasn't like this. He was no more than five years old when she died and from those little memories he had of his mother – almost abruptly, though affectionate – he knew that she was a lovely woman.

He looked at his mother as an idol until his father told him the reason of her suicide – which he had to believe; and that commenced an immense hatred for his own mother in his mind and maybe, that's why he hated Angel.

Angel was her sister and he protected her from everything which could harm her until she turned three, until his mother died and until his father deceived him about his mother's death. He still remembered how he and Angie bonded together against all odds which were laid by his father and how his uncle helped them get out of it. When he first found out about her boyfriend, Anshul Bhatt, the first thing he did was a background check on Ansh. The reviews came good, and somewhere inside, he felt good for her. But then, he had to oppose her in obeisance to his father. He didn't like abusing and insulting his uncle whom he saw as an inspiration while growing up; but then he had to. He was pleased to hear that his uncle was setting the date between Ansh and Angie; but then he wasn't the only one who had heard his uncle's conversation, his father too was standing behind him and at his behest he had to go with his friends with hockey sticks and bats just to show his father. He wasn't going to harm both of them and luckily, Dhruv came there and gave him the excuse of returning. He never felt offended by Dhruv's insults, neither had he hated him. In fact, had he been in Dhruv's place, he would have done exactly what he did, and he admired Dhruv for that. He knew Dhruv was an irresponsible spoiled brat, but could go to any extent for his friends and he believed that's the characteristic of a good person. He certainly didn't like Vishal. In fact, he hated him for trying to kill his uncle. He didn't like to fight Dhruv at the hospital, but then he had to. He knew this was going all wrong, but then he thought she deserved to suffer, as his father suffered because of his mother. He was somehow pleased to see Dhruv there on her engagement. He was watching them from a distance and was pleased when Mr. Shah was taking her away. He already knew what they were there for; while his uncle and auntie were packing their bags, he had gone home and had seen them. But instead of telling his father, he waited for them to take his sister away. He didn't want to intervene and stop them while they were leaving, but when his father stared at him with fuming red eyes, he had to obey him. He didn't charge back at Dhruv not that he couldn't, but he thought being seen defeated would ensure freedom for his sister, a sister he loved secretly but couldn't protect openly.

Mrs. Shah came with a white paper and handed it to Rishi. Angie was observing her brother as he was reading it. First his eyes went wide, astonished, then tears started falling from his eyes. By the end, he was growling and squeaking in pain.

"This is…" His voice chocked, leaving him unable to finish his words.

"Her suicide letter. She wasn't the one who cheated; your father was shamelessly disregarding every single vow of their marriage. He was someone you can call a molester, abuser, beater, cheater - everything. She committed suicide just to get rid of him. She loved you, but perhaps her love for you was overshadowed by her sufferings. This letter was kept away from you because of your father and my father who was as helpless as he is now," said Mr. Shah, putting his hand on his shoulder and within no time, he broke into his uncle's arms.

Angie was still surprised to see everything. Rishi then turned towards her and held her hand.

"Please forgive me, truffle!" A single word, within no time, brought tears to her eyes. This is what he used to call her before he started hating her; when he used to take her out for walks, when he was her guardian angel and how could he forget that it was Rishi who gave her the name – Angel.

"It's okay Rishi Bhai! I don't blame you, especially after knowing all of this." She caressed her brother's hair and hugged him. She felt stronger now, and experienced the same feelings she had when she used to play with him, when she used to be a little princess of her brother.

"I promise you truffle, I promise you, I'll get him back." He offered firmly, but his voice was grouchy because of crying.

"No need of that Bhai. I have you now, which is a bigger reason to celebrate."

She rubbed Rishi's back; he was finding it hard to stop his sobs. She then went to the kitchen and came back with a glass of water.

After an hour or two, Rishi stood up to leave, promising to come back the next day. He said it would be impossible for him to stay with his father anymore but Mr. Shah made him realise that he was now the only one who could run his family business and to keep his father away from destroying it. That he was the last ray of hope for their family and he had to stay there to look after his company.

On their convocation day, Ansh and Angie were finding it hard to face each other and were sitting far from each other, which brought a big gossip meat for their peers. However, at the time of lunch in the campus mess, Dhruv sitting beside Angie instead of Ansh was a bigger topic of gossip.

"You should probably be sitting with him. You're catching more eyes than me, Dhruv!" Angie suggested.

"Since when did you start worrying about other people, my friend? Or maybe you don't. You're worried about him aren't you?" He muzzled.

Angie shrugged off the words.

"You know, there's no point lying to you! So, now you know why I'm telling you should be sitting with him. He looks quite angry about this."

"I'm not giving him what he wants Angie. I'm giving him what he needs. Besides, he has Shilpan, Aakash and Harsh with him."

Angie was playing hide-and-seek with Ansh's eyes. Dhruv who had no intention to interrupt them was eating his meal when his phone beeped.

"Nirali?"

"Hmm…"

"So, finally, huh?"

"Nothing like that Angie, she's just a friend."

"I was told – of course by you – that you loved her, right?"

"I was fifteen then. Right now, I'm in love with your best friend only."

"So if I want you to be in love with her, I might have to make her my best friend?" Quipped Angie who didn't know then that every single word would come true afterwards.

Even after lunch, everyone was unable to leave the campus mess due to heavy rain. Ansh was standing at a distance with his eyes lingering on Angie. They were clearly missing their moments in rain, and Angie, for whom her entire future was shoved in absurdity, was standing alongside Dhruv who was looking after her just the way M had.

Had M been in her place, what would she have done? Just wait for him to come back to him?

No, she would have advised her otherwise. M had just made one mistake which had caused her a distance of seven months from Dhruv. After that, M told her many times not to wait for things to come back. If it doesn't, then it never will. She tried to think what would it be like to have her around? What would she tell her?

And she had her answer. She was going to talk to him and finish it once and for all – either way. She walked up to Ansh and Dhruv followed her; she was standing before the person she loved and she wasn't going to be weak. She knew what she had in her mind and she said it.

"So, having fun, Ansh? By beating around the bush? By insulting everything your friends and my dad did for us? I left my own engagement for you and I thought you'd be standing there instead of your friends to receive me! But you know what? You never wanted me in the first place. It was I who was after you madly. But now, it's enough! If you don't want to talk to me, then it's fine! From now on, I'll never cross your way; and I wish that makes you happy," Angie cried out, leaving Ansh embarrassed before everyone who was gathered around.

She then handed her bag to Dhruv and said, "Dhruv I'm going, please keep my bag. I'll take it from you later."

She started walking in the rain, taking slow and attentive steps, her dress was soaked and her mascara was all over her cheeks, mainly because of her tears. She kept walking until she felt a force was holding her hand. She knew who he was; she could remember his touch even in the greatest oblivion. He possessed her hand, and she felt he was going to conquer her – again. The thought put an instant smile on her face.

"Excuse me ma'am, can you tell me the way to the examination hall please?" His voice came from behind her; she didn't move, she wanted him to turn her around, with his hands on her shoulder and then...her back.

"Sorry, but I'm not going in that direction," she answered playfully with a shy grin.

"How about a walk? To wherever you're going!" Ansh was yet making no effort to move her and she felt mildly annoyed – as she badly wanted to see him.

"I don't think you trust me enough to walk along with you, sir!" Within no time, his tongue was probing her mouth and as she was deprived of it, she made no attempt to hold back. He finally won her over and their love story was completed. The funny part was that she never thought that they would kiss in middle of their campus; but it didn't matter now...they had their degrees with them.

"Angie?"

"Hmm?"

"Is it the rain or your boobs are getting softer?" He quipped.

Boys will be boys, whenever they kiss a girl, touching breasts is the next thing on their mind.

She punched him hard on his chest and a sound of applause moved their attention; they saw Dhruv standing there, the only eyewitness for all their ups and down – perhaps the only living one.

"Should I send you an invitation card to join us?"Ansh shouted out.

"No, I thought I might wait until you finish your Boobjob!" Dhruv retorted with a big grin and eventually ended up running, with both Ansh and Angie trailing him with a punch.

As Ansh was asked to press a horn while he reached Angie's home, he did accordingly and Angie finished all the preparations for their welcome. She was running here and there to make everything perfect. Mr. Shah noticed her and warned, "Hold your exhilaration princess, no need for any hurry." She knew he was right, but then, she was an Indian bride who was going to turn her love marriage into an arranged one. She had to look perfect.

Ansh entered along with his parents, they shook hands with Angie's parents and Angie was in a dilemma whether to touch their feet or not, but in the end, she did, putting a smirk on Ansh and Mr. Shah's face.

Greetings were done, welcome drinks and snacks were served and they were settled to discuss further course of action.

"So, when should we tie their knot?" Mr. Shah was the first one to break the ice.

"I think in their mid-internship will be better, they'll have the chance to focus on their pre PG entrance,"Mr. Bhatt, Anshul's dad replied.

"Exactly, and I think Angel needs it more than Ansh,"muzzled her mother. Angie sighed in disapproval.

"Sir, before we go any further, I want to clarify that we have a condition,"Ansh interrupted. Angie felt a crushing force nudged deep down in her heart. *'What? A condition? Where did this come from?'* She thought.

"Son, I and her mom left my company, and our house to bring together you two. I don't think I can give you anything more, but still, I'll try to fulfil your demands, for my daughter's sake. So tell me what is it?"Mr. Shah said in disappointment.

Angie had never seen her father helpless; perhaps hurt, angry, disappointed...but never helpless, that too because of her. She decided in her mind that if it was anything like dowry – even with its mere chances – she would call it off.

"My father will brief you about this. Over to you, dad!"

Ansh's father picked up his bag and pulled out some papers and a brochure, placing it before Mr. Shah.

"As you know, our house is not adequate for two couples, so we were looking for a bigger home, and there is this four BHK bungalow we have planned to buy." He explained, leaving Angie's family stunned and somewhere inside furious.

"Four BHK? That must be a costly affair!"Mr. Shah said, trying his best to keep calm.

"That's why we have come to you, Mr. Shah!"

Angie was about to burst, but Ansh through his eyes pleaded her to remain calm, which she did, hoping for all of this to be a nightmare and was waiting for someone to come at rescue and interrupt the conversation.

"What can I do in that, Mr. Bhatt?"

"Well, we've decided to move there before their marriage. Alone, I can't afford that house so we want your help in that. We want both families to shift there, so we can plan better for their marriage. Here is the detail of home loans, we can share EMIs of that house and together, we can afford that house," Ansh's dad blasted.

Angie and her mom-dad had their jaw dropped open. This was beyond their wildest imagination.

"What???? You want both our families to live together?" Mr. Shah asked in disbelief.

"Yes, Mr. Shah. Ansh came up with this idea and like you, I too found it weird and illogical. But then, he left me with no choice. He proposed this condition to me before you and I could have agreed to it." He explained and Mr. Shah turned to Ansh who was smiling.

"Ansh, I appreciate your affection, but you don't have to do this for us,"Mr. Shah started and Ansh held his hand high to interrupt, poured himself some water and cleared his throat before he explained. "Sir, by this, I'm not returning any kind of favour to you. I know this looks mentally and practically irregular and in one word, crazy, but I was duty-bound to do this and the same condition I had put before my father when I told him about Angie. Now it's up to you whether you accept me with this or not."

Angie was ambivalently looking at Ansh and Mr. Shah simultaneously but unable to understand the uncanny condition her boyfriend had brought up.

Her father gazed at her and asked, "What do you think about this?"

Angie's heart echoed, *'I badly want this dad!'* but she remained silent. He then looked at his wife and as she knew her daughter's wish better than anyone, she nodded with a smile.

"Okay then, if it's your final decision, then let's work on the finance." He shrugged and picked up the papers. Angie, who had just witnessed a historical moment needed to go somewhere alone to celebrate it with herself and she stood up.

"Should I make some coffee for everyone?" She offered.

"I'll help her in that," Ansh voluntarily stood up.

They both headed towards the kitchen and the first thing they did there was a luscious kiss. She kept rewarding Ansh with her kisses for making this happen.

"When did you plan all of this, Anshu?" She asked, with her head on his chest.

"The day you moved here." He kissed her head.

"What? I thought you didn't want to see my face then. You were so miffed at me!" Angie said, moving her fingers through his head and finally giving him an opportunity to kiss it.

"Was I? Who told you that?" muzzled Ansh and brushed her lower lip with his tongue before entering her mouth. The kiss lasted for several minutes and luckily, no one came there to interrupt them.

"Angie!"

"Hmm!"

"I need to tell you something." She didn't look up, and remained still in his arms.

"Hmm?"

"This wasn't my idea."

"What?" She looked up, straight into his eyes.

"M, she took a promise from me. No one – not even Gajju – knows about it. She knew that dad will have to leave his home for you and she said, 'When that comes up, you'll have to make this wacky yet amazing thing happen'. I was just simply trying to keep a promise I gave to her." Angie burst into tears as she heard it; her best friend did this from her deathbed? She was indeed a genius and after this, Angie knew she'll never be able to find enough words to thank her. Not just Dhruv, she had made her life special too.

Ansh who too was having tears in his eyes, kissed her cheeks.

"I was planning to propose you in a different way after the convocation, but since you left me embarrassed and afraid before the whole campus, I didn't have any choice left." He chuckled.

"Oh poor baby! I'm sorry! I…I…didn't know what to do then. I was so annoyed by your constant ignorance!" She put both her palms on his head and kissed his forehead.

"It's okay, my love! Alas, this was bound to happen."

And then, together they remembered their best friend M, who was now among the stars and just like Dhruv, they too were feeling her hand on their heads from the sky.

No one, not even god can write a perfect end for you! Unless he's dying.

Epilogue

I Dhruv Gajjar, am sitting along with my best friends, Ansh and Angie, who just postponed their honeymoon for me; and the love of my life, Nirali, who pulled me out from a deep sludge and made me realise the value of my life, which I'd completely lost after M. And M, how can I forget that genius? When Ansh first told me about the promise she took from him, I had nothing apart from tears to offer. Angie was right, from her deathbed, she had made our lives special; but what is it that was bothering her?

"What is it Nilu? It's been fifteen minutes since I finished my narration and you're just sitting pale?"

"Dhruv, Ansh, Angie, I don't know what my future will be with you all after this, but I have to tell you something. But before I speak, I want to tell you that you guys mean an entire world to me and like you three, I too was bound to a few promises," replies Nilu.

What? Promises? From whom?

She grabs her purse and pulls out two envelopes from it. Wait! I've seen them somewhere…Oh my…How did she have them? Yes, same sky blue and purple envelopes which M had asked me not to touch.

"How do you have these envelopes?"I snap. Realising that my gaze makes her uncomfortable, I move my eyes away from her.

She holds my hand and says, "It's better if I read these letters out to you."

The three of us nodded and she opened the first letter.

Dear Nirali,

First of all, I want to thank you. Inadvertently, since you brought the most special gift in my life, Dhruv Gajjar. Yes, I'm his girlfriend. M*****. I don't know whether you know it or not but you were his first crush – to be precise, his first love. He always saw a shadow of you inside me. He used to say, the only difference between us is your specs. My intention of writing this mail to you is not to narrate our love story. Actually, I'm not his everlasting love; not anymore. We are not breaking up either. Actually I did, because I don't want him to know that I'm dying. Yes, what you read is true, I'm dying. I'm in the final stage of Neurofibrosarcoma – a peripheral nerve sheath tumour. The tumour cells are rapidly spreading to every part of my body and eventually they will eat my body and free my soul. Only I know how I'm managing to type this mail to you. But before I die, I want to do something extraordinary for him. Something that no one has ever done for any one, not even in any book or any film and for that, I need your help. I'm following your updates on Facebook for a while and from there I got your email id. If you had and still have feelings for him, then reply to my mail; but only if you are sure about your feelings.

Our eyes are widened like saucers, what in the holy lord's name was that? A mail from M! It nudged deep inside my heart and perhaps she knows it too. She knew that my reaction to this would be absurd and that's why she didn't tell me. But then, how can I be angry at something related to M? I took her hand in mine and kissed it to give her the strength she needed – just the way she has done all my life.

"Go on Nilu. I'm with you and nothing is going to change between us after that," I said.

She cleared her throat.

"Then I met her, we had a lot in common. It didn't take long for us to be friends and I bonded with her parents also. Dhruv, I can't compare myself with her because she loved you with a different passion. We both loved each other, but we had that fear of rejection; she didn't. I still remember her words:

"Nirali you know it's not easy for me. I really don't want to go. If I had a chance to be with him, I would. I don't want to share his love with you or anyone and I mean it. But I have to do this hard job. I had to end the curse on my family here. I can't see Dhruv sacrificing all his life looking after me where I'm on a wheelchair, waiting for my death. Even if I undergo surgery and sever off my leg, the cancer will come again. It will not stop coming till I leave my body. I've seen my grandfather dying with the same disease and I know how it will retaliate. I know Dhruv, he will give up everything to look after me, and I'm going to die anyway. I'm going to die sooner or later, but I don't want to leave a depressed and good for nothing boyfriend behind. I'm doing this because he is not going to see a girl ever unless I send one for him. And I choose you. You were his love and he still has feelings for you, I've seen that and now I understand why – because of the person you are. I'm not imposing anything on you against your will; take your time, assure your feelings and decide. You don't have to indulge yourself into anything just because I'm dying. It is going to be your decision.'

"She was not only your best friend, guys; she became my best friend too. You know Dhruv, we used to play a game, that who knows you better? And she was quite annoyed when I used to defeat her every time – because I've seen you growing up, my love. Of course I know you better than her, but if not more than me, I know she loved you the way I do."

She looks up to catch me smiling. I'm feeling loved, by the praises I have just got from the two girls I fell in love with – despite being the nerd I was and still am.

"She never told this to anyone else; she was always cheerful and we felt like she was enjoying her death," said Angie in tears. But wait, is she being jealous?

"I know she said that she could share her pain, possessiveness and fears only with me. She had to be strong in front of you all and her parents; she feared you all would break down. Our meetings used to last for hours where I would just sit and listen and try to absorb some wisdom from her. When Dhruv introduced me to you all, I was quite exhilarated because I already knew each one of you by her words, especially you Angie. She told me everything about how you and Ansh were making out upstairs – in the name of study – and how hard it was for Dhruv and her to restrain themselves." She answers and I see Angie blushing with her wet eyes. Ansh wraps his arms around her, allowing her to cry.

"Her mom and dad?" I ask.

"I met them yesterday, they're missing you."

"I miss them too."

"Don't be disheartened, my love! They are being looked after – and that too, without breaking your promise." She's right, through my better half they are, and will be looked after and I'm not breaking my promise. Take that, M!

She blinks her twinkled eyes and tightens her grip on my hand and I realise that I'm holding it for very long.

"Anything more?" I ask.

"Just one thing…" She says, tears the second sky blue envelope and pulls out a paper and hands it to me.

"This is for you, and she strictly told me not to read it before you."

But before I start reading, Ansh stops me.

"Gajju, you are allowed to see her pictures only once, right?"

"Yes, why?"

"If you are fine with it, I think on the projectors upstairs, we should relive all those moments, for one last time."

"You have those pictures with you right now?" He nods.

Righteously so, I too want to see her now. Ansh and Angie have a beyond perfect end of their love story, my book is about to finish and I've fallen in love again – all that because of her. We need and deserve to see her, I wanted to save it for later but there will be no other moment like this. I may end up with a dusted image of her in my later life but she'll always live and be remembered in our memories. Yes, we will spend the night in the excursion of our memories.

"Okay buddy, now, may I?" I ask; somehow I don't know why I'm nervous.

I open the letter and yes, I feel amused by seeing her handwriting – for one last time.

●

Hey Mithu!

Surprised? No, stunned right? If you are reading this that means I've succeeded in my mission. You and Nirali are together. See, as I promised I sent a girl for you. What did you say? Don't make the promises you can't keep. See, I kept my promise. You must be wondering, when did I write this letter? After taking promises from you? No, long before that; and don't pressurize your mind on thinking how I know you'd say it, it takes a genius like me to know it (wink). You may have outsmarted me so many times, but you will never be able to beat me after this. So, by outsmarting you for the last time, I win. Ya ya you can smile, grin, smirk, use each word of your choice, but you can't change the fact that I'm smarter – from where you are reading this – let's say I was. Hey mithu! don't cry... stop I was just kidding my love! Okay I give up – let them out, once and for all.

By the way, how are Ansh and Angie? I'm sure you succeeded in reconciling them and I know you all are stumped by the end I planned for them. Ansh did it right? Say my "hi" to them and don't forget to gift them that silk scarf as a honeymoon gift from my side.

So, tell me, are you going to miss me? Yes, you are. I bet you all are; but I'm not going to miss you guys. I know I'm lying, but let me think what I'm going to miss the most. Yes, I got it, our romantic walk on Galway, Ireland. Remember? Just like you, I've dreamed of it so many times. I'm going to miss that the most. Didn't I tell you to stop crying? Oh c'mon Mithu, shedding tears won't bring me back! You have me right there. Yes, look inside your girl's eyes, you'll see me there. Now what you are going to do is that you'll take us to Ireland, take a walk just as we discussed, and don't you dare to make out there; that you promised me. I can't share my moments with anyone else, not even with Nirali. Yes, I can share you with her – by having no other choice – but not our memories…they are mine, forever. And don't worry, I did not die virgin in my dreams (wink again). So, it's time to say goodbye then.

Goodbye, my love! Kisses and hugs, over and… Dead (Oops, sorry baby just kidding! don't get angry now! huh…)

P.S: I'll always be with you – and you know that.

Coming soon by the same author

Everything We Had

Mausami Hansraj idolizes the characters in *Keeping the Promises*. She is the most loved Radio Jock of the city and a strong-headed person, hard to win. Her friends know it would take an equally strong-headed person to win her heart and respect.

Anmol Sahni, probably the richest man of the city and a fan of Mausami's voice, is not all that fortunate. Even with all the money and riches, there is little he can do about the inherited disease of the nerve cells that is slowly taking life out of him.

Oblivious of the fact that his condition is worsening faster than he anticipated, he allows himself to fall in love with Mausami. But both of them are realists, and part their ways as Anmol decides to die in solitude.

She gives in to his promise; she decides to honour her word despite all the devastation it is bound to cause. But as every coin has two sides, every philosphy has two ways, every wisdom has two different impacts, promises also have two sides. She accidently stumbles upon the very people she idolizes from *Keeping the Promises*, only to realize that their life is nothing like she has hoped all along.

Mysterious events with their presence in her life lead her to hate the people she idolized once. She decides to show the world that life is too surprising for a person to anticipate one's fate.

Thus, she tells her story, and in the loving memory of her everlasting love, she names it, 'EVERYTHING WE HAD'.

www.ingramcontent.com/pod-product-compliance
Lightning Source LLC
Chambersburg PA
CBHW071208260626
47162CB00004B/1214